A doctor and writer who traversed continents long before a pandemic brought our worlds to a standstill, Padmashree Mukand taps into both the scientific and creative spirit. Born in India, Dr. Karl Shergill carved an inspiring career across medicine and literature. After earning his MBBS and becoming a Fellow of the Royal College of Physicians of Ireland, he lent his talents to the NHS—all while cultivating parallel passions for poetry and prose. The author of over 10 books and plays that have garnered acclaim in Punjabi and English, his writing often explores the immigrant experience and what it means to heal others as well as ourselves. From early-career accolades like the Garden Party at Buckingham Palace to researching GI disorders to recently translating his own novel into a second tongue, Dr. Karl Shergill's works reflect the vision of a citizen at home in the world. His observations lend insight and empathy equally into the consulting room and the human condition.

Previous works:

Pandhravan Lal Cross (Fifteenth Crossover), short story collection in Punjabi, 1990

Hun Main Ajnabi Nahin (I Am Stranger No More), poetry collection in Punjabi, 2019

Kaun Suturdhar (Who Is The Creator), poetry collection in Punjabi, 2021

Lockdown Alpha, novel in Punjabi, 2022

Lockdown Alpha, novel translated into English, 2023

Dedicated to the characters in this novel who struggled to live their lives and maintain their human relationships through the COVID-19 pandemic.

Karl Shergill

LOCKDOWN ALPHA

(signature)

AUSTIN MACAULEY PUBLISHERS™

LONDON • CAMBRIDGE • NEW YORK • SHARJAH

A CIP catalogue record for this title is available from the British Library.

ISBN 9781035826735 (Paperback)
ISBN 9781035826742 (ePub e-book)

www.austinmacauley.com

First Published 2024
Austin Macauley Publishers Ltd®
1 Canada Square
Canary Wharf
London
E14 5AA

Thanks to my writer friends and my family who gave me valuable suggestions during the three-year period during which I wrote this novel. I thank the editors and proof readers and cover designers of this book. I would also like to thank the production and admin team of Austin Macauley Publishers.

Lockdown

"I'm afraid I won't be able to meet today," Amrita informed on her mobile.

"Why not?" Karan asked.

"Don't you know?"

"I don't."

"I am sure you remember the announcement by the government yesterday?"

"I don't remember."

"Do you remember your English wife's name?"

"I don't remember."

"It sounds like you are losing your memory; you seem to be suffering from dementia. May I suggest you eat five soaked almonds in the morning? These are supposed to improve memory."

"Why not ten?"

"No, only five. Ten will increase your cholesterol. But don't worry, I won't let you die because I do Karvachauth fast every year for you."

"What is Karvachauth?"

"Well, have you even forgotten that? You made a big mistake emigrating to England. You seem to have overlooked Punjabi culture and traditions. Dear Karan, you may remember women keep this fast for the longevity of their husbands.

"Why for me? Why not for your husband, Manav?"

"Because you are the real love in my life, my dear. How often have I told you that I only love you and no one else in this universe? I sincerely live for you and my life will end with you," Amrita again said without hesitation.

Karan became silent as always, listening to this repetition. He started shuddering, realising his extramarital friendship with Amrita was improper.

"Why do you go silent when I express my love for you? Well, when are you going back to the UK?"

"When I can get a flight back. Due to lockdown, most airlines have cancelled their flights," Karan informed her.

"There is a lockdown in place in Punjab, but the public does not care. I heard that the government is thinking of imposing a curfew. Why don't you stop here in Amritsar until the COVID pandemic is over? I have heard COVID is much more prevalent in the UK compared to India. Many people are dying there. You are much safer here," Amrita advised Karan.

Karan was already aware of these facts. He was in a dilemma about whether to stay in India or return to England. Amrita was right about rising cases in the UK, especially among the elderly. It was fatal in those with a suppressed immune system due to predisposing diseases and who were on chemotherapy. They were more likely to die. National Health Service UK was under pressure due to a lack more doctors and nurses. Quite a few of them had COVID and were in quarantine at home or admitted to hospitals.

Therefore, his hospital was more in need of Karan and he wanted to return immediately but could not due to travel restrictions. There were some last minutes flights to lift stranded British citizens.

Karen abruptly stopped talking to Amrita on the phone. He remembered his wife Jessica and son Theo. Both doctors in hospitals were fighting the Coronavirus on the front line. The fear of being unable to catch the flight back to the UK and be with his family made him increasingly anxious. He remembered Jessica's beautiful and proud face.

His son Theo rang, instructing him, "Dad, come back home and catch any next flight. If Air India has stopped the flights, catch other flights. There will soon be a complete restriction of overseas fights to the UK, dad, don't delay, just come home, we need you, Mum needs you."

While in India, Karen often met Amrita and her husband, Manav. They were lifelong friends from their college days. Despite being married to Manav, she remained very much in love with Karan. Karan had difficulty understanding his relationship with Amrita and how to handle this.

He felt indebted to her love towards him and did not want to upset her for not meeting her. But he always felt uneasy after meeting her and ashamed of himself for having an odd relationship. The whole situation confused him. He reached out for a shot of whiskey from the bar and quickly downed it. He got angry with himself and shouted in desperation, "Oh, my God! I shouldn't be meeting Amrita at all. It is morally wrong."

He then called Amrita to tell her their friendship was over forever. But before he could do that, Amrita was on the phone.

"I know you're in a hurry to go back to England. I have heard Corona is spreading like wildfire in the UK. I think you are safe here with me. If you want to go, there is just one last

11

Air India leaving at one pm tomorrow from Amritsar airport to London. I have asked my travel agent that if you want to catch this flight, pack up your luggage tomorrow morning, collect your ticket from the travel agent and arrive at eleven in the morning. If you do decide to go, then "Goodbye! Love you forever!"

"Goodbye forever," he muttered to himself.

The next day, he arrived at Amritsar airport two hours before the flight. He headed towards departures and then to check-in desks. There was no one behind any desk. The entire airport was empty. He went to the Air India office to inquire about the flight. The officer in charge informed him, "The Air India flight departed at ten in the morning before the international flight restrictions by airport authorities due to lockdown. The Air India flight was the last and there will be no more flights for at least a month."

"Why was I not informed of this? I am sure someone could have contacted me via text message or mobile phone," he shouted, but no one noticed him.

Extremely disappointed, he took a taxi back to the travel agent. He discussed the situation with him. The agent then searched for flights by other airlines to the UK on the computer. He found an alternative fight.

He informed Karan, "Luckily, there is just one last British Airways flight departing tonight at 2 o'clock from Delhi for London. I have also found one connecting flight from Amritsar to Delhi. I can book it, but considering the circumstances, I cannot guarantee the flight will go ahead. In case the flight is cancelled, there will be no refund. You may get a refund for your Air India flight. I am afraid it is a costly ticket and will cost you twelve hundred pounds, one-way economy class. Would you like me to book it?"

"Yes, of course, please go ahead" Karan had no choice but to buy this expensive ticket.

"Good luck. I have also booked a connecting flight from Amritsar to Delhi, leaving at 5 PM today."

Karan collected the tickets and went straight to Amritsar airport. He boarded the flight to Delhi airport. He arrived at Delhi airport and went through immigration. The immigration officer checked on the computer. Unfortunately, his name did not appear on the passenger list for the London flight. He became upset again.

In desperation, he phoned his old friend, the head of Delhi airport security. He sent two officers who took him to the British airway check-in desk. The officers took the ticket from him. They went straight to the desk. The check-in clerk informed them that passengers needed to confirm their seats before going through immigration and security.

After confirming his seat, the security officers took him back through immigration. Then, after clearing security, they took him to the VIP lounge to rest until the flight's departure to London.

Karan felt relieved. He had something to eat and downed it with a red wine. The VIP lounge was busy with business people from different countries and other Indian states. They were all busy talking on their mobile phones, looking very worried. Most airlines were cancelling flights. Everyone was anxious to reach their destination somehow. All passengers were constantly looking at the flight information board. Some were sitting in the bar, eating and drinking. A few were trying to sleep in comfortable chairs.

Karan phoned Jessica at home from his mobile phone to inform her. "I will be home by noon the next day. Please send Theo to pick me up from terminal five at Heathrow airport. He should check the arrival time of this flight before leaving."

"OK, love! I Miss you so much! Here Corona is taking its heavy toll. There are very few ventilator beds in the ICU. I am working long hours. As you know, there is no cure for this novel virus and the treatment for this is supportive with ventilators in ICU. Many patients are dying in front of us. Doctors and nurses can't do anything. They get very emotional at times and cry. Anyway, come and we can discuss this when you arrive. Have a safe journey back home." Jessica's voice was full of fear and helplessness.

"I miss you, my darling. I'll be back tomorrow. I'll text the flight number. OK See you tomorrow—bye."

Karan texted the flight number and tried to relax on the chair. He remained restless due to frequent cancellations of flights shown on the flight information board. He was repeatedly looking at the board for his flight. The British Airways plane had not yet landed. He was fearful that the plane might not arrive due to the lockdown.

Unfortunately, his fear came true. He looked at the flight information board and saw the flashing message, "British Airways Flight Cancelled."

The flight controller announced to passengers, "British Airways have not been able to take off from Heathrow airport due to the lockdown."

Karan could not believe this. He just stared at the board. He picked up his bag and ran to the booking desk at British Airways. The desk was empty and the notice board was showing, "London flight cancelled."

At first, he was outraged. Then he felt restless and experienced a panic attack. Holding his head, he sat down on a nearby bench. He tried to control his panic state by taking a deep breath. He drank some water from a bottle. The uneasiness subsided and he phoned his wife, Jessica.

"The flight has been cancelled. I will not be able to arrive tomorrow. Flights are grounded for a month but don't worry. I'll find an alternative route to come back somehow soon. Don't worry."

"Take care of yourself—try to come soon—I love you." Jessica was tearful.

"I love you too!" He kissed her on the phone and spoke, "Goodbye, my darling."

"Goodbye, see you soon."

"OK, but not OK."

Karan calmed down after calling Jessica. Jessica's voice had always been a comfort and strength for him. He looked at the flight information board. There was one flight leaving for Amritsar at six o'clock in the morning. He arrived at the domestic terminal with his luggage. Luckily, he got a seat on this flight. He checked through security and boarded the plane. He landed at Amritsar airport, all shattered.

He had to go through a public health checkup at the airport again. The public health worker measured the exact average forehead temperature. Non-Resident Indians were called NRIs in India. The Indian Government strictly instructed to quarantine any NRI from England in a secluded hotel for two weeks.

He explained he had returned from Delhi because British Airways had cancelled his flight to the UK. He also informed he was a doctor and knew the quarantine rules. He had no symptoms. The public health officer did not allow him to return home and sent him to a hotel used for quarantine. The health workers repeatedly subjected him to temperature and symptom checks in that hotel.

Although he was annoyed by the strict behaviour of public health officers but being a doctor, he understood that they were trying to prevent Corona spreading. By no rules did he need a quarantine. He spent one day in quarantine with incredible difficulty.

The next day, he rang Manav, head of the public health and nodal officer for pandemic prevention in Amritsar. Dr Manav came with his wife, Amrita. They convinced the public health officer that Dr Karan Singh did not need quarantine because of rules and regulations. Manav and Amrita brought their friend to his home.

Back to Amritsar

Unwillingly, Karan had to come back home to Amritsar. His family lived in a farmhouse on the outskirts of Amritsar. His parents, brother Harwant and his wife Ninder lived together in this house. The farmhouse had two pillars at the entrance which led to the hall, lobby, dining room, study, lounge and five bedrooms. Each bedroom had a washroom. A few years back, his parents moved here after selling their house near their business in the thick of the city. His parents fulfilled their ambition to live near their previous village.

Karan came back to his family again. They would generally have hugs and kisses, but they kept their social distance from each other. This time they greeted each other by folding their hands together and shouting aloud 'Sat Sri Akal,' meaning, "Truth is the timeless one."

Amrita and Manav were regular visitors to Karan's house and they always felt like a part of a family. They came with Karan to spend some time with him. Father and mother sat in the lobby to watch television. While others made themselves comfortable in the lounge. While sitting on the sofas, they all kept the required distance from each other.

"Didn't I say, Karan? It is safe here than in England," Amrita reminded amusingly.

"Yes, you did say, but I have my job to do in the UK. My patients there need me urgently."

"Would anyone like a cup of tea?" Ninder wanted to change the subject.

"No thanks, let's have some scotch instead. Our friend has been through a lot. He is troubled and distressed," Manav interrupted with a rare smile.

As always, Harwant got up and approached the bar in the corner of the lounge. He very reluctantly poured double measures of single malt whiskey and offered Karan and Manav. After a couple of drinks, all started exchanging their knowledge about COVID-19. Ninder brought some snacks and sat down next to them. Then began the conversation.

"COVID-19 or Coronavirus confirmed to have spread in Punjab in March 2021 when a Punjabi priest returning from Italy tested positive. I am sure everyone knows it first started in Wuhan, Hubei Province in China. In India, a Kerala student studying in Wuhan returned to India, which was the first case. More students arrived with positive tests from Wuhan. COVID then spread to Maharashtra, Mumbai, Delhi and Ahmedabad. So far, few cases in Punjab and very few in Amritsar," Manav informed.

"It's going to be a terrible pandemic. The World Health Organisation (WHO) should have declared an international emergency very early. It has already spread to many countries and has become a pandemic. There are approximately one and a half million cases of Corona in a hundred countries already leading to many deaths," Dr Amrita also shared her information.

Karan also spoke about COVID-19 in the UK. "It reached Europe through a businessman from Wuhan. Britain's

Foreign and Commonwealth Office banned travel to Wuhan in late January. Jessica has informed me that she has admitted many patients with COVID-19 infection to the hospitals. As you know, the treatment is mostly supportive with ventilators and quite a few patients are dying. The government is thinking of total lockdown alpha soon."

"You live in a rich country with excellent health care. Health care in this country is more private. Government hospitals do not have many modern facilities, such as sophisticated ventilators. Hospitals are running out of oxygen. I wish the communist parties would run this country. All this would have been a lot better here." Manav, as usual, started the political debate.

Karan was more of a conservative and he felt that the free market produces a better economy and jobs for the progress of any country. He believed in progressive evolution. Manav was a staunch communist and believed in Marxism and Maoism. He always thought India needed a revolution to topple the current government and the country run by the communist party.

Amrita believed India would be better off with a mixture of conservatism and socialism. A central policy based on the people's needs can lead to a country's progress. Whenever the argument between Manav and Karan became intense, she would logically interfere to stop further discussion.

She would not hesitate to rebuke them. "Why the hell do you both want to involve yourself in politics? For God's sake, you are both doctors. Remember the Hippocratic Oath, "I will use my power to help the sick to the best of my ability and judgement; I will abstain from harming or wronging any man. It would be sensible to devote your energy to your patients suffering from COVID and containing it. Come on, big leaders! Doing something better than debating something is not your field of speciality"."

They stopped for a while but started arguing again at the dinner table.

"Look, Manav, governing a great country like India, is unprecedented. India is now a developing country and does a good job of containing COVID-19 via lockdowns and curfews. I have heard 'Made in India' Covaxin is on the horizon and soon will be in people's arms.

"Now, with the open Indian market, the economy is growing. Once the economy grows in the free market, more people get jobs due to opportunities created by businesses, enterprises and the corporate sector. All this leads to social mobility. Social mobility from poverty to riches is already happening in India. Business and property become the property of the people who then feel valued.

"I come to India every year and can see progress everywhere every year. Its infrastructure, motorways, new airports and other means of transportation have vastly improved. I have noticed huge shopping malls and beautiful and luxurious homes for people, which brought real progress," Karan delivered his lecture without any hesitation.

Manav listened quietly, but his anguish became apparent in his statements. "I'm sorry, my friend! If India has made any progress, it is not due to capitalism. India has progressed due to socialism and the five-year plans adopted by Nehru, like Russia. In socialism, the government and workers share in businesses, industries, services and enterprises.

"This ownership inspires workers to work hard. Socialism believes in equality and the distribution of wealth amongst all classes of society. The government intervenes in the labour market and keeps it in check. In the free market, corporates try to pay workers the minimum wage and keep handsome profits for their shareholders."

"I think if India had embraced capitalism and the free market after Republic Day, it would have become as rich as Malaysia, Singapore and Western countries by now. The right ideology would have eradicated poverty," Karan spoke out of his conviction to conservatism.

Manav got angry because he couldn't agree to disagree and reached for another whiskey. Amrita snatched the bottle from his hand. Fuming, Manav left the table to go to the washroom and closed the door.

"Sorry, Amrita, I should have kept quiet today." Karan was feeling a bit embarrassed.

They became silent and then smiled at each other. Karan was feeling ashamed of the repetitive arguments. Amrita started telling Karan, "Manav has been drinking alcohol a lot more and is now taking hard drugs. I removed whiskey bottles and pills when I could find them. He is now becoming a secret alcoholic and druggy. His blood tests and liver scans point towards alcoholic-related early cirrhosis. He is ignoring my advice altogether. I need your help, Karan."

"Oh, God, yes—I saw his hands shaking. I will see and advise him."

"Promise me you will stop these political arguments with him from today."

Manav came out of the washroom and acknowledged his bad behaviour with his rare smile. "Sorry, everyone, don't worry. The bulls always fight when they are in the ring but remain friends after the fight. Amrita, let's go home now."

Harwant and the family took no notice of their habitual arguments. He informed Karan, "Yes, Amrita was right about Manav. He has become an alcoholic and a drug addict. I have heard he has started injecting morphine intravenously. He has been confiscating morphine from the hospital. The matter has reached the medical superintendent and he will be suspended from his post." Harwant, an ENT specialist in the same hospital, informed Karan.

"Well, he should not be working as a doctor. He feels like a frustrated communist, which may be the cause of his alcoholism and drug abuse. He needs to forget his ambition of bringing a revolution in India." Karan tried to scrutinise Manav's behaviour.

"It is also possible that it hurts him, knowing Amrita loves you more than him. She does not hide her love towards you. Whenever she visits us, she only talks about you. She always dreams of you coming back. She always dreams of you returning permanently and would love to receive you with open arms. Not being loved by his wife would have affected Manav's mental health and led to addiction."

"I have often told her that we are merely friends, but she takes no notice. I don't know what to do. I hope she looks after Manav and refers him to a liver specialist and rehabilitation," Karan expressed his helplessness.

The COVID-19 Pandemic and Lockdown Alpha

The COVID-19 pandemic was spreading more and more all over the world, including UK and India. A Chinese laboratory found early COVID-19 cases in Huanan Seafood Wholesale Market, selling live animals. A few patients and a doctor had symptoms of a novel virus: fever, dry cough and fatigue. The other symptoms included abdominal pain, vomiting, diarrhoea and sore throat with loss of taste combined with a loss of smell.

It affected elderly patients and those with certain underlying medical conditions. It is passed on from one person to the other when people breathe in air contaminated by droplets and small particles containing the virus. This virus spread to people who gathered at parties, meetings or concerts and were closed to others. The risk of living these was highest when. The novel virus was given the name COVID-19.

The world had difficulty controlling the virus because of its changing variants. It then became a pandemic in March 2020. It caused more than six and eight million cases and six and half million confirmed deaths, making it one of the deadliest pandemics in history.

Many countries introduced vaccines which prevented about 20 million deaths. Measures such as lockdowns, social distancing, wearing masks, improving ventilation and air filtration and quarantining also helped prevent the virus's spread. Treatments with monoclonal antibodies, novel antiviral drugs and steroids further helped control symptoms.

Many countries closed businesses and education institutes. The pandemic caused severe social and economic disruption worldwide and the recession. There was a food shortage all over the world.

World Health Organisation named variants using Greek letters and called the initial virus 'Alpha variant'. Then delta variant in India was no longer common. Various jurisdictions took more drastic actions, such as quarantining entire populations and strict travel bans.

Travel restrictions left many travellers to get stranded in other countries.

Love Triangle

By now, Karan was a cardiologist in England. Department of Public Health has appointed Manav as a professor at Amritsar medical college. Amrita became an anaesthetist and head of acute medicine and ICU in a private hospital in Amritsar.

Manav was madly in love with Amrita, but she did not love him. She got married to Manav because of an arranged marriage by their parents. After emigrating to the UK, Karan fell in love with Jessica. Amrita was madly in love with Karan and Manav got very hurt. It was one-sided but true love. She felt it in her heart, mind and soul. She worshipped Karen like God and often blamed herself for not showing enough devotion to her beloved.

Many psychologists believe that one-sided love is only for romance or friendship. Some think a one-sided affair often prevents heartbreak. Even if the other person wouldn't show any love or even betray, the one-sided lover will ignore and make some weird excuses to continue loving. They do it out of this fear of a break in the relationship.

They would visit their beloveds' residences again and again to have a glimpse or to meet them. They would love to hear the voice of their beloved all the time. If they cannot fulfil these desires, one-sided lovers would go after the person like a stalker and even cause physical or personal harm. The beloved one sometimes pretends to be in love. This kind of person would be after some benefit, which may be financial or sexual.

One-sided lovers, passionate and weak-hearted, will not feel remorse even in the face of deceit. Some will either dare not to tell the truth to anyone, leading to suffering from lifelong pain. When they realise the truth, one-sided lovers often have broken hearts. They would become sad and suffer from mental illness. Some will then commit suicide due to severe depression.

Thus, Amrita continued to live such a life even after her marriage to Manav. She was constantly ringing him to hear his voice. When he didn't answer her phone, she did wonder whether Karan loved her. She was suspicious of his false, pretentious, but she would ignore those. She constantly rang to tell him the story of her friend.

"Karan, you know my friend Seema. She fell in love with a fellow known as Dev. But he only wanted her for romance and sex. She truly loved him, but it was a one-sided love. Seema was mad in love. She ignored any advice to break the relationship with him. When she became pregnant with him, she proposed to him to marry her; Dev flatly refused. Seema became depressed and she killed him and herself."

"I am sure you wouldn't do such a thing," Karan asked.

"I wouldn't because I am truly and madly in love with you. You are not like Dev, are you? I know you love me and I will not stop worshipping you, even if you wouldn't love me. You are always on my mind. I always pray for your closeness or just listen to your sweet voice. But if you leave me, I will do what Seema did."

"Is this a threat?" Karan asked.

"I wouldn't ever kill you. By telling you this story, I only want to convince you how much I love you," Amrita answered.

To be in love with Karan was Amrita's most beautiful feeling; she would not want to break that lovely relationship. Whenever she had a chance, she loved to say, "Karan, I love you! I love you! My life began with your love and will end without it."

Home Coming to England

Karen was now stranded in Amritsar due to lockdown due to Corona pandemic. Curfew was also imposed in Punjab because people were not abiding by the lockdown rules. The government stopped flights from India to the UK and many other countries.

Karen had missed his last fights. Many Non-Resident Indians, known as NRIs from the UK, got stranded during this lockdown. Thankfully, they all had their second homes to spend holidays in India. Many business people were also stranded in India and their business was affected in the UK and abroad.

Karan was desperate to join his wife Jessica and son to fight Corona from the front line. They were both doctors. Karan rang the British High Commission in India several times for further information on how to return home.

He could only listen to a recorded message, "Special flights are being arranged to bring back all British citizens and those who have been granted permanent residency in the UK. Every stranded passenger will be informed where and when to catch the flight. Please register yourself online with Corporate Travel Management. These charter flights will lift you from Delhi, Mumbai, Goa, Chennai and Amritsar. These charted flights will start in April."

The UK government then scheduled extra flights from Amritsar in May. Karan got on the first plane in May 2020. After boarding the plane, he had a sigh of relief. While on the plane, Karan started reflecting on his experience in India.

He also was terrified over the consequences of the Corona pandemic. The lockdown alpha and the havoc it created played on his mind repeatedly. He requested scotch from the cabin attender to calm himself. After drinking and dinner, he relaxed in his seat and then started reflecting on his past, particularly his life in medical school.

Life at Medical College

When a person goes through a crisis, he tries to comfort himself with the lovely memories of the past. Karan often reminisced about his past, his old life and especially his days in medical college. He remembered the days of his medical college. Karan enjoyed his training for MBBS with his friends, Manav and Amrita. He would always admit those days were his life's sweetest and best days.

Every day, after lectures and teaching in the hospital, they would lunch in the canteen. In the evening, they would walk on Lawrence Road after playing hockey. Even during medical training, all students addressed each other as 'Doctor Saab'. Even walking or shopping, they would dress in a college blazer with a logo on the left-sided pocket to show off.

The schedule for training in the college was very tough but enjoyable. Karan remembered when he first entered in anatomy dissection hall. It stank of chloroform. It made every student's eye water due to chloroform irritating the eyes. The preserved human bodies were lying on marble-top tables. The public donated these bodies; some died on pavements without relatives or fixed addresses.

Medical students, in pairs, dissect the human body to study the anatomy of each part and organ. The knowledge was tested after the dissection of each part of the body every week. There were practical and theoretical examinations for all medical subjects. If not passed, then the exam would have to be retaken.

MBBS degree format was a replica of the British Raj days. The format in the UK had been modified and was much more straightforward. Instead of an examination in each subject, there was an exam of every speciality in one test. Yet, every student remained motivated to become a doctor and desired to cure patients.

Moreover, there was a kind of friendship and brotherhood amongst all the students to lift each other's morale when they felt low. They were happy within their group of friends and would create an atmosphere of laughter by cracking jokes and absurd tantrums.

Karan had a very close friendship with Manav and Amrita. He was popularly known as 'Hero' because he looked like a Bollywood Star. Karan was a very handsome six feet tall young man. He was a heartfelt and intelligent person. He was an atheist who believed people did not follow the religious teachings of equality.

Amrita was the most beautiful girl and looked stunningly like a model. She was fair-coloured, with glowing red and pink cheeks. She was tall and had a slender figure with a long neck. She had been 'Miss Medical College'. Her upper lip was a bit shorter and her upper two front teeth were more prominent; students often teased her as a 'bunny rabbit'.

She was habitually very talkative; once she started talking about any topic, it was difficult for her to stop. She was clever, with an incredible sense of discernment. She never hesitated to tell anyone off when they happened to harass her. Amrita, the princess with a very charismatic personality, was the only daughter of a royal family predating the British Raj. The royal family lived in a Royal Castle near Amritsar.

Every day, she would arrive at the college in a chauffeur-driven vintage Rolls Royce car and walk out of the vehicle with great dignity. She would walk through the rows of lovers waiting for her before entering the lecture rooms. Whenever anyone whistled at her or called her 'Bunny Rabbit', she would tell them off like a lioness. The only person she would feel shy from was Karan.

Manav and Karan were childhood friends. Both were from the same village. They both completed their premedical education together. Manav was an intelligent man with an extroverted personality. He didn't like the corrupt government and poverty in India. Manav was a bitter communist and had studied Karl Marx, Pushkin, Mao and many other communist writers thoroughly. He believed that only Marxism and Maoism could bring revolution in India with the power of a gun.

Even in medical college, he was becoming more and more associated with medical students of the same ideology. Karan never agreed with his extreme views; therefore, Manav kept his distance from him in the last few months of his final year in medical college.

Manav deeply loved Amrita, but she didn't love him because of his extreme leftist views. Still, Manav did not stop thrusting his love for Amrita. He followed her everywhere, like a stalker. Once during school days, all three went to see a movie. This film, 'Sangam', had a love triangle story. After the film show, Manav kept singing to her a love song from the movie to Amrita—"Bol Radha Bol Sangam Hoga Ke Nahi," which means tell me if you will love me or not.

And Amrita laughed it off, saying, "No—No—No!"

Manav's father was a retired army officer. Major Amarpal Singh owned a big farm. After retirement, he settled in his village. Major was not good at farming and therefore employed farmers from the neighbouring states of India, Uttar Pradesh and Bihar to work for him. Like other landlords, he had to keep up high-class appearances.

Therefore, in his farmhouse, it was essential to have a tractor, a jeep, a bullet motorcycle and a posh car. The outgoings of running the farm were more than the income; therefore, he had to borrow more money each year from banks. The livelihood of the family depended on his pension. The funds generated by the farm were just enough to pay off bank loans. The Major had taken over the village postmaster's job to make ends meet.

Being a retired army officer, Major wanted strict discipline at home, so he was very strict with the family, even on domestic matters. He was putting pressure on Manav to study hard to become a doctor. He also prevented him from meeting his friend Karan simply because he was from a different caste. Most of the time, his behaviour towards him was disgusting.

Therefore, Manav could not get along with his father and hated him. Whenever he met Manav and Karan together, Major would not hesitate to say, "I want Manav to work hard to become a doctor. Karan, you are distracting my son from achieving his goal and considering your intelligence, you can never become a doctor."

Final Year Examination

But it so happened Karan topped the class by getting top grades. So did Manav and Amrita. All three of them gained admission to medical college. They became much closer to each other, always studied together and sailed through all examinations. Amrita fell in love with Karan in those years, knowing he was from another caste and her parents would not allow her to marry him. Karan also kept her guessing about his feelings towards her because he knew Manav was deeply in love with Amrita.

The final year examinations for MBBS were coming up. Karan was a day scholar, meaning he lived with his family in their house in Amritsar. Manav and Amrita were regular visitors to Karan's house and would go out together. Karan's family treated them as their own.

Normally near every exam, Karan would move in with Manav in his student accommodation on the college premises. They always would study harder together. Karan didn't think staying with him this time was a good idea as Manav was captivated by his other communist friends and was becoming unfriendly towards him.

One day unexpectantly, Manav came to Karan's house and sat down with him. He said, "Come and stay with me, please. We will study together like we do every year for the exam. We work harder together."

Karan agreed hesitantly and asked him to coordinate his terms until the exam. He said, "Manav, you will not allow students or his poet friend who believed in extreme leftist ideologies to disturb us."

Manav agreed and Karan decided to move to his accommodation at medical college. Like every year, they started working hard to prepare for the final year of MBBS.

Manav, being deeply in love with Amrita, had difficulty concentrating. Every two to three hours, Amrita's name would come up, "Oh, my God, Karan, I can't live without Amrita," "I want to marry her as soon as we pass the finals," "But she does not love me. How can I make her love me?", "I know she loves you. Tell me what to do?"

"First of all, keep away from Marxist and Maoist believers. She is the daughter of a royal family and they do not like your revolution. Secondly, you take her out for dinner or a movie and express your feelings with love. You are also from a rich family. You are also from the same caste as Amrita. Both being from the army, your father and her father are best friends. Be nice to your father and ask him to arrange your marriage with her. I do not see any problem providing Amrita has no objection."

"But Amrita would not agree," Manav looked desperate.

"You know that a princess must agree to an arranged marriage by her parents. Royal families always look for a suitable husband. Once they find one, they ignore a girl's feelings. I am sure that is what is going to happen in the end." Karen was not hesitant to say that.

"You wouldn't mind—would you?"

35

"Why should I mind—Amrita's parents will not let it happen because I am from a different caste. You are from the same upper-class families. You are perfectly suited to each other."

This agreement silenced Manav and he smiled within his sleeves. He promised he would not keep going about Amrita anymore but concentrate on the examination. He said, "After the exam, I will start taking her out and show how much I love her and win her over. Let us get back to work and pass the finals."

As the final MBBS exam was near, all the medical students were anxious to pass. Tensions were rising high and some students were behaving absurdly. Someone would shout and say any number. Then the others would call random numbers, eighty-eight, ninety, hundred, for about five minutes.

After the shouting match of the numbers, there would be complete silence. Then a student who aspired to become a psychiatrist would scream as if he had been in agony. His neighbouring students would go to his room and find his most bizarre behaviour. He was pouring cold water on the floor with the fan and the heater. When asked why he was doing this, he said to ease his tension.

In addition to exam pressure, there was another pressure from the canteen waiter Sardara Singh, who would serve tea and food in students' rooms during an exam. He had made his list of students who would pass or fail. Nobody knew his list, but to be on the pass list, all students would pretend to work hard when he would bring morning tea or food. Everyone would recognise the sound of his footsteps and quickly start reading books.

Then the final year MBBS examination of all subjects started. A medical student, Parkash, who lived in the adjoining room, came in after taking the General Medicine practical examination. He was disappointed and he started telling Karan and Manav.

"Dudes, my viva has not gone well. They asked me to read an ECG tracing. It looked like normal sinus tachycardia but paroxysmal atrial tachycardia."

"It means you have to prepare for the next exam." Manav showed no sympathy.

"Parkash was not on my pass list, anyway." Sardara Singh, who was standing nearby, did not feel any pity.

"Don't worry. You will pass when examiners combine your theory and practical marks," Karan tried to encourage him.

When it came to Manav's turn for practicals, he became very nervous. In a panic, he declined to appear in his exam. Amrita persuaded him to go for it. Surprisingly he did well.

The exam was over and the university announced the results a month later. Karan, Manav and Amrita all passed MBBS and have doctor's degrees. Amrita passed the final examination with high colours by achieving the highest marks and became a gold medallist. Parkash also passed and the first person he told was Sardara Singh.

They all started doing a Punjabi bhangra dance in front of Sardara Singh. Another student, now a doctor, brought his Dholak drum and started playing bhangra beats. Seeing everyone happy, Sardara Singh also joined in and so did the girls.

Amrita was more excited and she kept dancing with Karan, but Manav kept coming in between them repeatedly.

Everyone who passed had great joy and pride in becoming a doctor after five years of the MBBS course. Everyone's face was glowing with happiness, like overflowing lava. Those few who did not pass were sad and stood on one side. Everyone went up to them and consoled them by saying they would pass in six weeks when they retook supplementary exams of a subject they failed.

Looking at them, Sardara Singh got his pass list out, tore it in front of them and brought them into the crowd. They then also joined in the bhangra dance to alleviate their disappointment. Six weeks later, they also had a supplemental final exam and they all passed.

Karan, Manav and Amrita went to a nearby restaurant to organise a big party for everyone after the degree ceremony. Amrita left early. Karan advised Manav how and when he should propose to her, "On the day of dinner after the degree ceremony, you should make this move. First, you show how much you love Amrita. Then at the dinner table, you sit to her left and I will be on the right. Don't start any silly political debate.

"Just compliment her beauty, dress, eyes, makeup and complexion. Then finally, hold her hand lovingly and softly say, "I love you, Amrita. I can't live without you. I want you in my life. Will you marry me?" If she agrees, show her your diamond ring and put it on her ring finger straight way."

"All right." Both showed thumbs up in agreement.

It Didn't Go as Planned

The degree ceremony was held at Guru Nanak Dev University in Amritsar. At the grand ceremony, Karan, Manav, Amrita and their classmates were conferred an MBBS degree by this university. After the ceremony was over, it was time for a celebration party together as planned. Karan had organised this in a hall of a hotel in Amritsar. They had dinner and a party afterward.

As planned, Karan and Manav sat on each side of Amrita at the dinner table. But Manav became very nervous and drank a shot of whiskey swiftly. He was eager for an opportunity to win over Amrita. He kept moving his chair near her and she kept moving towards Karan. After the dinner finished, Manav nervously grabbed Amrita's hand. Amrita tried to get his hand off. Contrary to the plan, Manav kneeled down in front of her with a diamond ring and proposed, "Amrita, I love you and want to marry you."

But Amrita stood up like a lioness. Karan knew what was coming, so he got up and tried to slip away from the table quietly. Releasing her arm from Manav, she stood in front of Karan, spreading her arms to stop his exit. Amrita raised Karan's arm and shouted in front of everyone, "I only love you, Karan and I can't live without you. I will only marry you."

Everyone applauded this announcement and the hall resounded with congratulatory clapping. They surrounded their table and joined in the spectacle. Manav tried to explain to Amrita the inevitability of her parents' disagreement, which would lead to a forced marriage with him.

Karan calmed down everyone and proclaimed, "Friends, as you know, Manav is in deep love with Amrita. They are suited to each other because they are from the same caste families. Infect their parents have already arranged their marriage. So, it is fair that they should get married. It will be marriage from heaven."

Amrita got very angry at Karan. She slapped Karan on the face and ran out of the hall. Karan and Manav followed her. The driver was waiting for Amrita. He opened the door of Royals Royce and Amrita angrily sat in the back seat. She allowed Manav to sit in the car and advised the driver to shut the door in Karan's face. She then ordered the driver to drive off to her home.

Karan asked her to open the glass window and tried to apologise. She looked the other way and Manav did not respond either. She started crying in the car and arrived home sobbing. Karan felt as if he had lost everything. He ran towards the car for a while, but the car speeded up and suddenly disappeared. Their whole story of friendship and love vanished in the cloud of dust created by a royal car.

Helpless Amrita

Amrita and Manav remain silent in the car. She kept sobbing in her home. Manav did not have the skills to handle this unprecedented situation. Once or twice, he tried to console her by repeating, "Everything is going to be all right—. believe me, I will look after you—I love you, Amrita."

She was fuming with anger and shouted at Manav, "What the hell do you mean—how it be all right? I don't even love you. So shut up, please."

Manav kept staring at Amrita. She looked more beautiful in anguish. He just wanted to hug and kiss her and console her with love. But the angry princess was not amused. He then reminded her of their already arranged marriage.

"It is no good crying; you know what's going to happen."

At this, Amrita started crying even louder. They arrived at the royal palace. The driver opened the doors of the car. First, to Amrita and then to Manav, entered the palace's front door. Her dad, Colonel Kanwar Pratap Singh, has already prepared to celebrate their joy at becoming doctors. Manav's mum and dad had also arrived. The Colonel and the Major were drinking scotch and making plans for the wedding of Manav and Amrita.

Amrita's mother, overwhelmed with joy, came to the hallway to fetch them. But seeing the tears in Amrita's eyes, she became sad. She took them to the big lounge. Both parents asked in one voice, "What happened to our lovely princess?"

The princess kept crying. Manav informed them what had happened. He also told them, "Amrita has been deeply in love with Karan and wanted to marry him."

Knowing this, Amrita's mum became very angry. She started abusing her and even hit her on the back with a stick she had in her hand.

"How could you even imagine marrying a subject from a different caste? Have you forgotten royal traditions? You don't care about the honour of your royal family?"

"No, I don't. This is my life and I will decide who I marry. I love Karan and will continue to do so. Hit me as much as you want. My life had started with loving Karan and will end with him."

After saying this, she ran to her bedroom and locked herself. Manav also informed Karan was not interested in Amrita and did not want to marry her. He made it clear, "I love Amrita and if everyone agrees, I am ready to marry her."

"Well, we have arranged your wedding, whether Amrita likes it or not. We, the parents, have no objections. Let's get the wedding date fixed soon. We were supposed to celebrate you becoming a doctor and declaring your arranged marriage today. I can't believe this is happening. She will have to agree to our arranged marriage."

Amrita had a good cry in her bedroom. She started reflecting on Karan's behaviour. She realised that Karan had never expressed his love for her. She became suspicious of his intentions.

Suddenly, she became aware that Karan did not want to marry her. Then there were family traditions and principles to be observed. She certainly did not believe in a caste system, but she felt Karan might have an inferiority complex. She thought this might be the main reason he declined to marry her. She was frightened of being alone if she did not marry Manav.

Then she started talking to herself, "Even if I marry Manav, I still want to keep in contact with Karan. I believe in my true love for Karan. My love for him is eternal and I don't want to let go of my relationship with Karan. Marrying Manav will let me keep that relationship through our friendship."

She arrived at her suitable decision and joined everyone at the decorated dining table for the celebration. She announced, "I will marry Manav in keeping with royal traditions."

No one could believe this sudden change in her mind. Amrita was an unpredictable character. She could change her mind after a quick reflection. She surprised everyone with her decision, but she had a hidden agenda.

Suddenly, sadness changed into happiness and celebrations. Manav lifted his whiskey glass as a toast to Amrita and so did Colonel and Major. All of them then started fixing the date for a wedding ceremony. Manav was thrilled. All sitting at the dinner table still could not believe Amrita and asked again, "Are you sure—Are you sure?"

"Yes, yes, yes!" she repeated.

Manav's Odd Thrills

Manav was thrilled and eager to tell Karan this good news. He drove on his motorbike to his college accommodation. Karan was packing to go back home. Manav stormed in half drunk. He had a bottle of whiskey in one hand and a pistol in the other. He was targeting Karan with a gun. Karan first got nervous and then started trembling with fear. But then he remembered an old incident during school days.

Manav was involved in the Naxalite movement. This movement started in Naxalbari village by the radical faction of the Marxist Communist Party of India. Its extreme left formed the Communist Party of India. They recruited students and launched widespread violence in West Bengal against the "class enemies" such as landlords, businessmen, university teachers, police officers and politicians.

This movement believed in bringing a revolution to India. Their purpose was to snatch rich people's wealth and give it to the poor. They were mercilessly killing people. This movement slowly spread to the northwest and to Punjab. The then prime minister, Indira Gandhi, declared the President's Emergency rule.

During this anti-insurgency operation, the army killed hundreds of naxalites and imprisoned many. This operation helped in declining violence. During that period, one day, Karan was sleeping in his house in the village. Even then, he came in with a pistol aimed at him. He was hungry because he was on a mission with other naxalites to kill a landlord of a nearby village. Their attempt was unsuccessful and the police were after them. He said, "Friend, don't worry. I'm not going to kill you."

"Then why are you aiming your pistol at me? Anyway, where did you get it from?"

"It is a gift from Chairman Mao of China, especially for me," he said jokingly. He put the pistol on the side desk.

"Who do you intend to kill now?"

"All the corrupt leaders and bring a revolution in India— Long live the revolution!"

They started debating Maoism, but Karan kept on making him understand, "You cannot bring a revolution with the power of the gun into a democratic system. The country needs good governance. Please, Manav, don't be fooled by this extreme ideology. It will finish you."

After remembering that incident, Karan became less nervous. He asked, "Let's have a shot of whiskey."

After a couple of drinks, Manav told Karan, "Amrita loves you, not me, but I love her. She seems to be very sensible about it. The good news is that our parents have fixed our wedding date. We will get married very soon. We will be inviting you to our wedding and you must come. You will, of course, be my best man. Start preparing the speech; it ought to be good."

"I am sure you and Amrita will have a happy married life. Congratulations!" Karan shook hands with Manav. He became rather emotional and hugged him, picked up his bags and said, "Bye, my friend. I won't stay here for your wedding."

"What do you mean?" Manav was surprised.

"I have decided to move to Delhi to do my internship. After the internship, I plan to leave for good and settle in the UK. I do not want to interfere in your married life. There is one thing, though."

"What?"

"Throw that Mao's revolver in the well."

"OK, as long as you promise to remain friends and keep in touch with us."

"OK, we will be in touch."

For the first time, Manav agreed with his friend. He assured him that he would return the revolver to a gun shop. In his mind, Manav murmured, "We will remain friends, but I will not get rid of this gun and change my ideology."

Emigration to the UK

Karan went to Delhi to do an internship. He could not believe that even close, intellectual and well-educated friends could destroy relationships due to social inequalities and caste systems. Karan often wondered whether the human brain is grown enough to mitigate discrimination.

A few months later, he learnt Manav was married to Amrita. Karan was not invited as a friend, let alone to be Manav's best man. Still, he was happy for Manav and Amrita. He felt they would enjoy married life without him being a part of a triangular relationship. Karan decided to stay away from them once and for all.

After marriage, Manav and Amrita decided to stay in the royal palace. To Karan, it was ironic that a communist lived as an imperialist.

Karan was now doing his internship in Delhi. He often missed Manav and Amrita but resisted making any contact with them. Karan knew Amrita would still want to see him, which would spoil their married life.

Occasionally, he felt lonely, but he was aware that loneliness could bring sadness. By reflecting on his past positively, Karan picked up his inner strength to do what was decided. Previously he had been in two minds about whether he should or should not go abroad, but after what had happened, he was determined to emigrate to another country. He chose the UK because he knew the English language and it would be easy for him to make his career as a heart specialist.

While completing his internship in Delhi, Karan learnt from the British High Commission about going to England and practising medicine. Karan had to pass the UK professional linguistic and assessment board in a short PLAB test. First, he had to apply to sit for this test at the General Medical Council of England and then after he got the date of examination in writing; he applied for a six-month tourist visa.

Karan had to prove he could meet the costs of exam fees and return tickets. He also needed sponsorship from someone living in the UK, which he got from his father's friend in the UK. The sponsor must provide evidence that he can accommodate, finance his living costs and provide health cover in case of illness.

He got an interview date at the British High Commission in Delhi. He prepared all the necessary documents and went for an interview. An English immigration officer interviewed him. He had a long face and a stiff upper lip. He was wearing half-thick glasses. He was an unpredictable gentleman. At the start of the interview, he continued scrutinising the documents and then started asking questions to Karan.

"Where will you be living in England?"

"I will be living with my father's friend."

"What does he do?"

"Businessman."

"You know how many children your sponsor has?"

"I don't know."

"Are you going to get married there?"

"I am going there to sit PLAB test. If I pass, I intend to make a carrier in medicine. If I am not successful, then I'll just come back."

"What does your father do?"

"Businessman."

"What is your home address?"

"Amritsar, Punjab."

"But there is a village address on the passport?"

"I was born there; I did my primary and secondary education there. I stayed with my grandfather in the village while all my family lived in Amritsar."

"What did your grandpa do?"

"A little bit of farming and business."

"What sort of business?"

"Buying and selling buffaloes and cows."

"How many cows, buffaloes and goats in your farm?"

"With due respect, sir, what has it got to do with the visa?" Karan got a little irritated by the irrelevant questions.

The interviewer looked at Karan for the first time, smiled and stamped a six-month tourist visa and said, "Good luck with your exam! I warn you, PLAB is a tough exam."

"Thank you, anyway, I realise that, but as I said before, if I fail, I'll come back."

After getting the visa, Karan started preparing for the exam. After completing his internship, he booked his flight to London. He packed up everything and a few days before the flight, he came home to say goodbye to his family at Amritsar. But his parents were distraught and did not want him to emigrate.

They all became very emotional and worried about his future. Karan reassured them that he would never forget them and would return soon after completing his degrees and specialist training. He wanted to meet and say a final goodbye to Amrita and Manav but did not consider it appropriate.

Amrita was informed, as usual, by his brother's wife about Karan when he was leaving for England. Amrita couldn't resist her feelings of seeing Karan off. The evening before departure, she arrived alone at Karan's house and, without hesitation, went straight to his bedroom, where he was packing his bags. Ninder asked her to sit in the lounge and that she will bring Karan downstairs, but she ignored her.

After forcefully opening Karan's bedroom door, she clung to him, hugged him, kissed him all over his face and said crying, "Karan, you know it was my forced marriage to Manav. I do not love him; I only love you and carry on loving you. Ours is the real marriage of our souls. My mind, body and soul will always want your divine love. You wouldn't believe I went to bed with Manav, imagining you with me.

"Forgive me. I have been unable to stand against this awful arranged marriage and caste system. You know I do not believe in these traditions and values. Please, Karan, do not leave this country and marry me. I can divorce Manav for you at any time."

"Stop, Amrita, stop. Are you crazy saying such things? You should be ashamed of this; now that you are married to Manav, you should respectfully accept him as your husband. He loves you and will make you happy. Wake up to reality," Karan tried to make her understand the whole situation. He had to separate Amrita from him forcefully.

"No matter how much you separate me physically, you wouldn't be able to separate my soul from yours. My soul will always haunt you."

Everyone had listened to their conversation. They already knew about this whole saga. Karan's Father ordered them to come downstairs.

"Karan—Amrita, come down. Cup of tea and cake are ready."

They both came downstairs to gather in the lounge to have tea. They all had tea. There was pin-drop silence in the lounge. To break the silence, father said some words of consolation, "Forget what happened in the past. Now you should be moving on. I wish all of you a happy life in the future. Always remember, what God does is always for the best."

"Yes, dear father," saying this, Amrita left the house with tears in her eyes. She did not even say goodbye to Karan.

London

The flight Karan boarded had one stop at the Dubai airport to refuel. There, all passengers moved to the departures. A ten-year-old Arabic boy tried to make conversation in Arabic. Karan couldn't understand what he was saying. He told him in English that he does not speak Arabic.

The boy kept saying something with his body language but got frustrated and stopped talking. Karan realised for the first time how important any language is for communication. The inability to communicate with the child made him emotional. Reading the expression on the child's face, Karan presumed he was saying, "Looks like you have left home for another country—good luck!"

At 6 PM, the plane landed at London Heathrow airport. After the ambiguous interview at British High Commission in Delhi, he was still anxious about whether the immigration officer at the airport would further question him. He arrived at the immigration officers' desk, who looked at every passport page. Finally started asking—"The purpose of coming to the UK?"

"To sit for the General Medical Council's PLAB test."

"When is the test?"

"On March the first."

The officer stamped his passport for a six-month stay. Handing over his passport, the officer wished him good luck. He breathed a sigh of relief.

After he picked up his luggage, he came out through the green lane. His father's friend Harjinder Singh was waiting in the arrival area with his wife Sara and daughter Jessica. Karan's father, Saheb Singh and Harjinder Singh were old friends when they had a garment import and export business. Harjinder Singh from London was importing garments from hosiery owned by Saheb Singh in Amritsar.

This business failed because of cheap imported garments from other countries like China and Bangladesh. Harjinder Singh started a property business in the UK and became a multimillion property dealer. He was now popularly known as 'Harry' in England.

Saheb Singh sold his business and vowed to make his sons professionals. They both remained very close friends. Harry would always visit him at Amritsar whenever he visited India. Harry owned several estates in the heart of London and had several flats in London and Hounslow. He had reserved one flat for Karan to accommodate.

When Karan came out, Jessica naturally recognised him.

"Karan?"

"Yes, I am Karan." He couldn't take his eyes off that beautiful girl.

"Did you have a good flight?"

"Yes, good, no problem!"

As soon as he saw Jessica, he felt lost. He was overwhelmed to see a thin, beautiful white girl. He sighed, panicked. Sarah asked, "Are you all right?"

"Yes, I'm good—I'm fine."

Harry took his suitcase and headed for a car park. A massive chauffeur-driven Bentley car was waiting for them. Harry sat in front and his wife, Jessica and Karan sat in the back seat. Jessica sat in the middle of the back seat next to Karan, a bit squeezed. He felt her body's warmth and was already in love with her.

Harry asked him, "How are your father and mother, OK?"

"Yes, they are fine, but they were very upset about me leaving them. I could not spend much time with them as I was in Delhi doing my medical internship."

"Are you a doctor?" Jessica asked him.

"Yeah—I can only work as a doctor in the UK if I pass the Professional and Linguistic Assessment Board in the short PLAB test. I have come here to sit for the test. General Medical Council very recently introduced it to international medical doctors. If I pass it, I will get a job as a junior doctor. I want to make my career in Cardiology."

"Good luck, Karan! Jessica is also becoming a doctor here in London," Sarah wished him well.

"Excellent—which year?" Karan looked at Jessica with a loving smile.

"Final Year—University College London," Jessica responded with a kind smile.

"Oh well, we can perhaps help each other," Karan said hesitatingly.

"Of course!" Jessica sounded excited.

The car journey from Heathrow airport to Hounslow was about five miles and took about thirty minutes. During the trip, Karen and Jessica became over-friendly and repeatedly looked at each other. They were talking about medicine courses. Karan explained the MBBS course format and so did Jessica. Jessica could speak some Punjabi, so their conversation took place in half English and half Punjabi. She asked him, "In which language do you study medicine in India?"

"In English."

"Then there should be no difficulty passing the General Medical Council examination."

"I am made aware that it is a challenging test—I have done a lot of preparation, though."

"Anyway—good luck."—Jessica patted Karan on the shoulder.

Engaged in conversation, they arrived at a flat in Hounslow. The apartment had a bedroom, an open-style kitchen, a dining room and a lounge area. Karan thought he was fortunate to be given such suitable accommodation. He thanked Harry, his wife, Sarah and Jessica. Jessica explained to him how to use the cooker, heating system, shower, lights and phone.

After this, Jessica and her parents went to their home in Richmond upon Thames. Richmond is about eight miles in Southwest of London. It is a very posh area with a low level of poverty. It is built on the banks of the river Thames. Nearby is the famous Kew Gardens, which hosts all kinds of botanical plants and trees worldwide.

Karan could only bring two hundred pounds legally from India. Harry, being aware of it, gave him another two hundred pounds. He told him to call him when he needed some more. Karan thanked him and then off they went home in the car. He kept looking at Jessica until the vehicle disappeared and Jessica waved him goodbye.

He returned to the flat and started unpacking and putting his clothes and toiletries in the proper places. Harry and the family bought some food items and put them in the fridge in the kitchen. Keeping in mind that Punjabis like their whiskey, he left one bottle of Black Label.

Karen was not expecting all that posh life but was grateful. He was thrilled to meet with Jessica. To celebrate this unexpected welcome, Karan poured a shot of whiskey into a glass with ice and drank it in one go. He was not that hungry but only ate half a sandwich. Karan started thinking about Jessica. He was very proud of himself for being very strong-minded, but the sensibility of love softened him. Karan felt love in his heart, mind and soul for the first time.

After another whiskey, he thoroughly enjoyed this love ecstasy and realised why people love poems and songs. He remembered Manav being in love with Amrita and he used to write love poetry to her. Amrita would also recite to him love poetry. She often told him love stories of Romeo and Juliet, Heer and Ranjha, Sohni and Mahiwal and Laila and Majnu. She would sing him Sufi songs. She loved Sufism and Sufi poetry. But at that time, he was not interested in anything like that.

During her college days, many other girls were after him to have a love affair with him, but he was just committed to becoming a doctor. After meeting Jessica, he felt love at first sight, but at the same time, he was afraid of his one-sided love for her.

Reflecting on his feelings, he murmured, "Oh, my God! Why have I let my heart feel like that? I don't know her and she may already have a boyfriend she loves. She is the daughter of a wealthy father. Why would she fall in love with him?"

He began to fear his one-sided love for Jessica, like that of Amrita and Manav. He just wanted to focus on passing his test. He felt embarrassed and had no choice but to go to bed. He was a bit restless but then fell asleep. He woke up in the morning, had a shower and then breakfast. He made up his mind that he would concentrate on preparing for the exam. He had just opened the book of multiple-choice questions when the phone rang. It was Jessica's phone.

"Good morning, Karan! Did you sleep well?

"Yes, thanks! I did after a couple of whiskeys."

"It's good. Dad left you a bottle of whiskey. Are you feeling settled though?"

"Yes, very well, no problem. Thanks for providing all these amenities. I am grateful."

"That's OK—take note of our home telephone number—call if you need any help."

Karan was over the moon to hear Jessica's voice. He wanted to tell Jessica that he had fallen in her, but he resisted expressing his feelings sensibly. Karan took note of the telephone phone number given by Jessica. He felt a hint of love towards him in Jessica's voice. When she went off the phone, Karan somersaulted like a monkey in happiness and joy. He took a breath of fresh air, standing on the balcony. He returned to the lounge, picked up the book and tried to focus but failed.

"Love shows different colours and love between two people is the beautiful feeling of surrendering to each other. True love does not differentiate between rich and poor, the colour of the skin, caste or creed." Karan realised his feelings towards Jessica was reality.

Really in Love

After he settled in the flat and he wanted to visit London. But he was not familiar with the places to visit in London. He had heard about underground railways but did not know how to use them. He would only go to a corner grocery shop nearby to buy milk, eggs and bread.

He was very reluctant to go out and about because of shyness in a different country. He didn't even visit Hounslow town. He remembered a female medical student gifting him a baby dummy on his birthday because he was a bit shy then. Since then, he has shunned his shyness and has become a forthcoming personality. He phoned Harjinder Singh to say he wanted to see London and wondered if someone could escort him.

The winter weather in the UK was frequently changeable. It was usually grey and cloudy, but it was a sunny weekend. He got a phone call from Harry that Jessica would show him around London that weekend. He was overjoyed with happiness to hear this. He eagerly waited for Saturday. Jessica came in her luxurious sports car in the late morning. She sounded the car horn to call Karan out of the flat. He was wearing bright casual clothes and she complimented him as soon as she saw him.

"Karan! You look brilliant."

"You, too, look gorgeous, Jessica." Karan was amazed at his courage to exchange compliments.

"This is the first time I've heard a compliment from a Punjabi boy. I know Punjabi boys do not know how to give compliments to girls. They would say in Punjabi—Hai way sohanio, sannoo vi bula lao kadi meaning hello beautiful, give us a chance to talk to you." They both laughed.

Jessica looked extremely happy that day. He took Karan on a trip to London. They visited Parliament, Buckingham Palace, Madame Tussauds and the London Museum. Finally, they had dinner in Chinatown. There talked about past life in schools and colleges. Then Jessica asked, "Any girlfriends or marriage?"

"No, no, I am not so lucky. In medical college, girls first look at how rich the family in which they are going to marry is. The girls always had some chip on their shoulders. They would rather look at the stars than the boys. Yes, there was a girl whom I consider my only friend. Her name was Amrita. She married my dear friend Manav, who loves her very much."

Karan gave Jessica a sweet smile and then asked, "Have you any boyfriend?"

"No, my dad, being Punjabi, is very strict. He often warned me that he would break my legs if I went out with any boy. Many boys had shown interest in me. There was a Punjabi boy in college who just kept following me. Sometimes he would follow me to the house. All he could say was, 'Kinda. Jess, which just meant, how are you?'

"Another tall Punjabi guy who was also known as Professor—he would try to grab my arm at the end of a class,

I would release my arm and grab the white boys' hand, then he would become jealous."

"My God—they sound very backwards."

"But today I was surprised when Dad asked me to go with you happily," told Jessica with mischievous eyes and added, "My dad seems to like you very much."

"And you?" asked Karan.

"I like you too," Jessica said lovingly.

They held each other's hands. They both felt the warmth of love. They stared at each other for a long and then Karan took the courage to admit, "I fell in love with your first sight at the airport." Karan could not resist saying that.

"Me too!" Jessica could not hold back her feeling.

They both kissed each other on the lips. Asians usually kiss on the cheek and it surprised Jessica that Karan kissed her on the lips. As night fell, the streetlights came on and the darkness disappeared. They imagined it was their powerful love which lightened the night. Enjoying every moment of joy, they arrived at the flat.

Jessica proposed, "Won't you invite me in for a coffee?"

"Of course."

They tried to make coffee but ended up kissing and hugging each other. They ended up lying in bed and made love and shouted again and again—"I love you, Jess"—"I love you, Karan"—"I love you!"

Karen and Jessica were in deep love, but they had to part and wait for the next opportunity to be close together.

Jessica returned home late in the ecstasy of love.

Money Shortage

Karan now had a minimal amount of money left. He was embarrassed to ask Jessica's dad for money again and could not get money transferred quickly from India. One day when he went to the corner shop to buy milk, he met two friends from Amritsar who were qualified as dentists and had come to take the dentistry exam, just like him.

"Bally—Harvey?"

"Karan?"

Karen was so happy to meet his friends from Amritsar Dental College in the corner shop. They were so excited to meet each other that they could not stop hugging. Meeting someone from your own country in a foreign land was like meeting your own family. Harvey also lived in rented accommodation in Hounslow. He had arranged marriage to a British Punjabi girl in the UK and therefore came to England with a spouse visa.

After about a year, his wife eloped with a white man; she had been in love with him. Harvey was hurt, but he was glad he got rid of her, as he had found out about her love affair. Bally and Harvey were preparing for a dental examination before they could practise. To pay for a living, Harvey was doing odd jobs in London.

Bally was lucky and married his wife, Jatinder, a property businessman's daughter. She was charming and beautiful. She gave him her full support to Bally. After marriage, Bally lived with his in-laws. He had no problem settling in. He had already taken dental but was not that lucky to get through.

"We have a lot to talk about our past and present. Let's go to the pub!" suggested Bally.

Karan and Harvey made it clear that they had very little money.

"Don't worry, today's drink and meal are on me," said Bally.

"One day, we will all have money and a grand party," Harvey announced his wish.

They all sat in Bally's car and drove to a pub in Richmond-on-Thames on the riverbank. It was a wonderful place. They sat outside the pub on wooden benches and drank beer and whisky. Then they started reflecting on their days in college. They remembered funny times and incidents and laughed over them. Bally was eager to share his funny love story again.

Bally fell in love with one of his class fellows, Kamal. It was one-sided love; therefore, Kamal did not show any interest in him. Bally expressed his one-sided love to Kamal many times, but she always ignored him. One-sided love drove him crazy and he didn't know what to do. Bally planned a crazy scheme to win her over.

He put on the long saffron robe, disguised as a historical lover and camped at the main gate of the dental college. He declared a hunger strike until Kamal promised to marry him. This scheme didn't work. He continued the hunger strike but could not tolerate hunger after a few days. After the dental college closure in the evening, he would go to the Golden Temple and eat from free Langar.

On the way back, like some Guru, he would keep chanting, "'Alakh Niranjan' meaning 'perceived creature' used by yogis" Passersby started believing him as a yogi and would bow to him to pay their respect. He got used to it, carried on with the hunger strike and introduced himself as 'Saint Romeo'.

One day when he was chanting 'Kamal—Kamal', someone came from behind and flogged him with a rubber slipper on the head. He jumped, woke up and looked up. He saw his dad with a slipper in his hand and the college principal standing behind him.

Several students were also around, all giggling and laughing at this spectacle. Kamal drove by on his scooter. The principal told his dad the girl who just drove by was Kamal. Dad struck two more blows on his shoulders and said, "I cannot believe you like that girl without any charm."

They all laughed at this absurd story and could not stop laughing, saying, "Such was his life of fun."

They had drinks and ate pub food. Then Karan could not resist telling his story. He also told his friends about his love story with Jessica and muttered, "I never dreamed I would fall in love with such a beautiful white girl. She looks like an angel and God has made her just for me. I thank God for Jessica to come into my life. I love her and it was love at first sight."

"Sounds like you too are in love." They all laughed.

They enjoyed this unexpected get-together and promised to meet regularly. Karan asked Harvey, "What is this odd job that you do? I need the money. Could you please take me with you?"

"Yes, Karan, but odd jobs are tough and manual labour. You will have to stand as a labourer and may or may not get the job. You must have seen a labourer standing in Amritsar Rattan Singh Roundabout; if you want, come with me and we will stand with labourers in Earl Court, London. The odd jobs are generally heavy lifting, packing and building work. You get paid an hourly rate at the end of day's job."

The following day, Harvey took Karan to Earls Court. They made themselves available by standing in the crowd of labourers. As usual, a moon-faced white man with central obesity arrived in his big Jaguar. He came out and pointed his index finger towards the workers and selected them for each van, which was taking them for different odd jobs.

Quite a few were left and one could see the disappointment on their faces. They were worried about how they were going to feed their family. Harvey and Karan were lucky to get a job in a warehouse for a week. This job involved loading heavy toiletry items into lorries and trucks. They both earned thirty pounds each in a week. Harvey was used to tough odd jobs. But Karan had never done such jobs. Even after wearing gloves, he suffered blisters on his hands.

After one week, Karan decided not to go back to odd jobs. Harvey didn't care; he was a qualified dentist and kept working because he needed money for his livelihood and to pay for the exams. Bally would sometimes help him. There was a sense of brotherhood between them, like in Amritsar.

Thames Manor

That Saturday, Jessica phoned Karan.

"Where have you been all week—you haven't picked up the phone?"

"Sorry, dear, I spent a week doing odd jobs because I needed money. So, I went to do odd jobs in London every day." He shared his situation with Jessica as if she was already his wife.

"Why didn't you ask us for money? Dad will be furious to know that," Jessica told him sympathetically.

That same day, Jessica, her dad and her mum visited Karan.

"It must be fun to do odd jobs; no worries, Son, I had to do similar jobs on my arrival to this country." Harry was happy that Karan had the same experience as him when he came to England.

"Silly Karan, look at your hands," Jessica showed her sympathy.

"Chal Banh Apna samaan," which means pack your belongings as we will take you to our house now, Harry laughed and said sweetly.

Everyone packed up his belongings and loaded them in the car. They arrived in Richmond at Harry's mansion. The name of the villa was 'Thames Manor'. It was a luxurious home with lights twinkling on the side of a half-mile drive. It had a beautiful entrance with long marble pillars in front of the carport.

The wide entrance door led to a long hallway, a vast lounge, swimming pool, bar, a cinema house, a modern kitchen with an island for breakfast on the ground floor and at least ten bedrooms on the first floor. At the back, it had a vast garden which extended to the banks of the Thames River. Flowing the Thames with boats and river cruises going about created fantastic scenery. As soon as they entered the mansion, Karan got excited.

"Wow! What a wonderful house!"

"Yes, it is a mansion, not just a house—my dad worked very hard to get where we all are. I am very proud of Dad for building his property empire in London. Well done, Dad," Jessica admiringly padded his dad's back.

Jessica took him to his guest bedroom upstairs. It was a big bedroom with a double bed in it. Jessica clapped and the lights came on. She clapped again and the curtains opened. Large windows with double doors in the middle led to the large balcony overlooking the Thames; the view was breathtaking.

"This is your bedroom now—hope you like it."

"I wonder why this king-size bed is just for me?" Karan tried to be cheeky.

"Well, from now on, you are not alone in your bedroom, my dear Karan," Jessica responded the same way.

"Thank you, Jessica!" he hugged Jessica tightly.

"Oh well, you don't have to do odd jobs anymore." She looked at his blistered hands and kissed them.

"Dinner is ready," Sarah shouted from the dining room downstairs.

They came to eat in the dining room. Karan enjoyed homemade Punjabi food, which Harry himself prepared. After dinner, they sat in the cinema room. They all watched the old Bollywood Hindi movie 'Sangam' with cations in English. It was Harry's favourite film and he had watched it repeatedly.

Sarah was not impressed with the Bollywood film and, as usual, she went to her bedroom. She preferred to sleep in a separate bedroom lately. Watching Sangam, this movie reminded Karan of Amrita and Manav. They saw this movie together quite a few times as well. Manav used to sing Amrita a song, "One day, I will get you and take you away and onlookers will be pleasantly surprised."

Karan started reflecting on his past in his mind. 'Past remains as a memory in one's subconscious mind. The conscious mind only taps into it when a similar situation happens. The subconscious mind remains silent, like a memory chip in a computer. It stores all the good and bad accidents of life as memories. Many sorrows and joys thus become a part of life. But to be happy, one could either delete bad memories from the subconscious brain or archive them in the unconscious mind, a technique used in psychotherapy with the help of Yoga.'

"Where are you and what are you thinking?" Harry shook Karan's shoulder.

"Nothing, just old memories of India," Karan said cautiously.

"Don't worry—every NRI suffers from this nostalgia, which slowly withers away. Here, something to drink will help you forget your past." Harry offered him to drink.

Karan drank a shot of whiskey and murmured, "Only if it does—I hope so."

He went to his bedroom, still thinking of Amrita and Manav.

Love Grew More Stronger

The love between Jessica and Karan grew stronger and stronger with each day. When Jessica would arrive home from college, she would go straight to Karan's bedroom to feed him English food like pork pie and pastries. He disliked English food and wanted to eat curries, dals and samosas.

Every Sunday, Jessica would take him to Southall. It would make him happy to be in Punjabi Diaspora. There were Punjabi grocers, clothing, sweets, books, Indian vegetable shops, Punjabi travel agents and restaurants. They would eat kebabs, prawns, dals, chupatis, parathas and samosas from restaurants and dhaba.

Jessica spent most of the evenings and weekends with Karen in his bedroom. Sarah and Harry, by now, realised the growing love between them and that they could not stay away from each other. Jessica was spending less and less time with Sarah in the kitchen. She was used to her daughter's company, which was no longer there and she started missing her daughter. Harry did not want to spoil the love between the two and make Jessica unhappy.

Sarah felt lonely; therefore, she began spending most of her time at their business office in London. She was a one-third partner in Harry's business. The company also had another third Irish partner. His name was Michael and he looked after marketing. Sarah was the financial director.

Sarah and Harry were worried about Jessica getting pregnant. One day Sara shared her worry with Harry. "I'm worried about Jessica and I had a good look in her bedroom. It doesn't look like she's taking any contraceptives!" Sara informed.

"Look, Sarah! Both love each other a lot, why don't we get them married?"

"That is an excellent idea." They both agreed and decided to ask them.

Harry called a meeting between Jessica, Karan, Sarah and himself in the bar area. First, they only talked to Jessica alone. Mum and Dad asked her, "Jess! Do you love Karan?"

"Yes, dad! By now, you must have known!"

"Does Karan love you?" Sarah asked.

"Yes, Mum!" Jessica replied happily.

"OK, now go and bring Karan down. We want to know from him," Harry ordered gently.

Jessica brought him down. Harry smiled slightly and asked Karan to sit in front of them. Karan got nervous.

"Don't worry!" Harry reassured.

"Tell me, Have I made any mistake?" Karan asked politely.

"No, tell me, do you love Jessica?" Harry asked bluntly.

"Yes, I love her very much." He took the courage to say this firmly.

"We're thinking of marrying you. Will you marry my daughter Jessica?" Sarah proposed.

"Of course, I do, but I want my parents' approval too." Karan wanted to discuss his decision with his parents first.

"Son, don't worry. I've already talked to your parents; I want to know whether you agree," Harry informed.

"Then it is OK from me too!" Karan accepted the proposal happily.

Jessica hugged Karan and they kissed each other. They were all happy and kept hugging their parents again and again. They opened a bottle of champagne and celebrated the occasion. Harry was eager to soon to fix the wedding date. Karan wanted to invite his family from India and expressed concern about his upcoming test and Jessica's course. Harry and Sara said together.

"Just postpone your test until after the wedding and I can take a few months out," Jessica suggested and kissed Karan again.

Postponing Karan's exam and Jessica's course was a good idea. Karan and Jessica felt relieved. Karan rang his parents and discussed his exam and wedding plans. They were over the moon with happiness to hear the good news.

Wedding Preparations

Considering it was a Punjabi wedding, preparation began the day Karan and Jessica agreed. The General Medical Council gave another date and postponed the exam for six months. He also extended his visa for a further six months. Jessica also applied for three months, which University College Hospital accepted.

Harry was excited as if he was already waiting for this wedding. He kept saying, "Punjabi wedding ceremony should start at least a week before marriage. This wedding is my opportunity to show off my daughter's grand, traditional Punjabi wedding. All my rich Sikh friends had grand, vibrant and extravagant ceremonies. I am going to have an even more grand wedding. Our Sikh community is fun-loving but has strong traditional values.

"Therefore, we should start wedding preparations now in advance. I will hire the most expensive and luxurious hotels for various ceremonies for each ritual. I will invite all my rich friends, relatives and VIPs from India, including film stars and famous Punjabi singers from Bollywood."

The wedding preparation began. Dad booked venues for the engagement, pre-wedding reception and Gurdwara for religious weddings and big receptions. Jessica and Karen wrote a program itinerary leading to the wedding day. The family then designed wedding invitation cards for printing and prepared a list of guests. An invitation card, a gift and Indian sweets were packed in a beautiful box and delivered to all guests at their houses personally and by post.

It was customary to send the first invitation to Karan's parents. Harry sent the first invitation to Karan's father, mother, brother and sister-in-law. They arrived well in advance to take part in preparations. Karan also wanted to invite Amrita and Manav, but he knew Jessica wouldn't like it. When he mentioned this to Jessica, she gave him a disgusting look. She did not want any disruption in their wedding ceremony. No matter how modern and open-minded a woman was, she would not tolerate old flames burning the most beautiful feelings in her life.

In any case, Karan did not insist on inviting them. Karan's family naturally stayed at the Thames Mansion as there were plenty of rooms. It was a pleasure for both families to be fully involved. Harjinder Singh was thrilled to have his friend Saheb Singh. The families felt united under one roof and the celebration started every day in the bar.

Sarah was also very excited about the wedding. She had attended many extravagant Punjabi wedding ceremonies; therefore, she was familiar with all the Punjabi wedding customs and traditions. Sarah was beautiful and used to be efficient as Harry's business secretary. She was much younger than Harry.

Gradually, Harry and Sarah fell in love and they got married. After the marriage, Sarah naturally became Harry's business partner looking after all company's financial affairs.

Harry's first wife, Sharan, was from Punjab. She came a few years after Harry came to England and worked in a foundry. She also worked hard in the laundry to earn money in England. They both worked very hard, saved money and slowly started their own business in garment manufacturing. When this business failed, they created a property business. But when they achieved success and it was time for happiness, she had lung tuberculosis which had invaded her bone marrow.

Despite anti-tubercular treatment, she did not recover and eventually died. Harry had a son Sukhbir from her, who remained in India to look after a big farm which Harry had bought. During these auspicious days, Harry was missing her and his son and sometimes he would remember her with grief and say, "Oh, my dear Sharan, you only saw hard-working bad days. I wish you were here now to share this happiness."

His son Sukhbir was born in Punjab. He was living in a sizeable villa-type house in a village in Punjab that his father got built. He graduated from Agriculture University, Ludhiana City in Punjab. He, therefore, knew the modern technologies applied to farming, which had brought Green Revolution to Punjab. Harry often visited him in Punjab and liked to spend his break from business there twice a year.

Sukhbir was not entirely happy about his father marrying a white woman younger than his age. He, too, wanted to settle in England with his father. He was also in love with his housemaid from a very low caste. But his father would not allow him to marry her. After Harry's marriage to Sarah, he did not visit Sukhbir. Sukhbir took this opportunity to marry his girlfriend without informing his father.

Harry invited Sukhbir to the wedding. He also arrived without his wife in the UK on a visitor visa. He was pleased to meet his family and Jessica. Jessica was over the moon to meet her half-brother. She thought he was very handsome but did not understand his rural Punjabi accent. Still, Jessica welcomed her half-brother with open arms. She was also happy having Karan's parents, brother Harwant and his wife, Ninder. Harwant was as tall as Karan and very handsome.

Harwant was an Ear Nose Throat surgeon in Amritsar. He spoke posh Punjabi and behaved like a professional doctor. He was generally reticent but would show off his knowledge and wisdom in discussions after a couple of shots of whiskey. His wife, Ninder, was a bit naïve but knew how to talk to others down when required. Accepting Karan's family as her in-laws, she looked after them as her own family.

Jessica had difficulty communicating with Sukhbir because he could not speak English and she talked to him in her broken Punjabi. Jessica tried to tell him, "Sukhbir main tenu bahut miss karda," meaning I miss you so much.

"Par Mera Burha menu mis nahin karda!" (My old man never missed me!) Sukhbir sighted disappointment in his father by addressing his father as Burha.

"What does Burha mean?" Jessica asked Karan, standing next to him.

"An old man in English!" said Karan.

"My dad is not a Burha. He looks so young." Jessica didn't like the comments about her father.

"Sukhbir does not mean age. In Punjab, country folks usually call their father Burha, Bappu, Bhaiya, Papaji and many more synonyms. But Burha is sometimes used as the rude word for father," Harwant explained politely.

"Harwant, too siddha ho key kaon nahin baith sakda, lagda jive tery bund te foray nikaley hundey," meaning why can't you sit straight? You sit on the sofa as if you have boils on your buttocks! Sukhbir was making a joke in rude Punjabi.

"What did you say?" Jessica asked.

"Sukhbir is saying that Harwant should sit straight," Karan tried to stop a further conversation.

"What is Foray?" Jessica wanted to understand.

"Foray means boils on the bomb, which does not let me sit straight. Rest assured, I have no boil on my buttocks," Harwant explained.

They all laughed and tried to make Sukhbir laugh, but he didn't get it.

They then planned to visit London before the wedding ceremonies got started. Karan, Sukhbir, Harwant and Ninder went to London underground the following day. By now, Karan was familiar with using underground trains. They had a tourist bus which showed them all the site scenes. While touring, Sukhbir sat next to Karan and Karan asked him, "Sukhbir, how is the village life and farming?"

"Dr Saheb, we have a big farm and I am doing well in farming. My Burha has built a big house there as well. I keep myself busy in agriculture. Business is fine," said Sukhbir.

"Why don't you address your father with regard as Bhapaji or even Dad instead of the Burha, which is quite a rude word," Karan said instinctively.

"Doc, when you live in a village, you pick up rural Punjabi. No one taught us posh Punjabi. Even at Agriculture University, all students were from farming families and they spoke my sort of language. I call him old man spitefully because he married a white woman younger than his age, soon after my mother died but would not let me marry my maid?" Sukhbir opened.

"Sukhbir, times have changed. You shouldn't be angry if your dad has a happy life with Sarah," Karan advised.

"Doc, I have also come to see my father's face because I miss him. I also want to know whether he is a multimillionaire businessman. When he goes to Punjab, he shows off as if he is the king or an emperor," Sukhbir put forward his hidden agenda.

"How is your girlfriend?" Karan changed the topic.

"Yes, she is good. I have married her and we are pleased to live together in our house. Please don't tell my dad. He might cause trouble during your wedding," Sukhbir told Karan everything.

"I think your father probably knows about it. He had no objection to Jessica marrying me," Karan said.

"I am surprised. We should celebrate it as the triumph of love. One thing is sure. It fills my heart with joy to look at beautiful Jessica. It is also a great pleasure to know my sister is marrying a gentleman doctor like you, Karan. Congratulations Doc, you are very fortunate." Sukhbir let his hidden wisdom flow.

"Thank you! How do you feel about Sarah?"

"I can't talk to her much because I cannot speak English. She gives me a funny look and I feel she is not happy seeing us at the wedding," Sukhbir replied reluctantly.

For a while, they remain silent. Sukhbir then asked, "How much do you think my father is worth in terms of his business and money?"

"I also have just come from India; I don't know anything about this. Perhaps you could explore it with your father after the wedding," Karan suggested, but this enquiry surprised him.

"OK, Doc, I will explore it."

Sukhbir Couldn't Wait

The following day when they all sat at the dinner table. Sukhbir asked his father, this time showing some respect, "Bhapaji! Can I ask something from you?"

"Of course, dear son!" Harjinder Singh responded with love.

"Looking at your mansion, estates and business, how much you think you are worth. You seem to be a multimillionaire in terms of money." Sukhbir could not wait.

"Yes, son, your father has built an empire with hard work. When I came to this country, I could bring only two pounds I borrowed from Karan's father and, with hard work with your mother, I slowly built up my business. You have done very well on our farm in our village and you are also worth a lot." Harry showed off his pride by saying this.

"I know you are in good health now, but have you done your will? Who are you leaving all your empire? I should have my share in your estate," Sukhbir asked without any hesitancy.

Everyone was amazed and silent, but Harry's face turned red with anger. He could not believe that anyone, especially Sukhbir, would demand his share in the will. Sarah didn't understand what they were discussing in Punjabi. But she could guess some curious talk was going on. She came up to Harry and held his hand and asked, "What's up, Harry dear! Why are you so upset?"

Harry told Sukhbir off before answering Sarah, "Look, son! I have not aged yet and I will not die tomorrow. You shouldn't have done this when we are all happy and looking forward to the wedding."

Hearing all this, they all felt stressed and got up from the dining table. Sukhbir ran to his bedroom. Everyone else went to the bar. They poured some brandy to calm themselves down. Harry told everything to Sarah. He got angry and shouted, "Stupid son has no sense when to open his mouth. I wanted to keep the secret that I have already given him all the assets in India in my will."

Karan's father, Saheb Singh, looked at Harjinder Singh and said, "If you have already done this, tell him that. He will be happy and will enjoy the wedding."

"Saheb, I have just been silly. You are right. I don't need to keep this secret from him. You go upstairs and tell him everything and bring him down." Harjinder Singh had cooled down.

Saheb Singh went upstairs and told Sukhbir, "Your father had already given you the farm and house in the village in his will."

Sukhbir was delighted to hear that. He was so happy he did not even ask about UK's property.

"Now be happy and come down. Let's celebrate your inheritance." Saheb Singh patted him on his shoulder.

"Why didn't he tell me this when I asked," Sukhbir asked with a smile.

"Your father didn't want to tell this in front of everyone, especially Sarah. He did not let Sarah have any assets in your village estate. He did this well before marrying her," Saheb Singh was trying to get Sukhbir to understand.

Sukhbir understood and came down with Saheb Singh. As soon as he came down, he touched his father's feet and begged forgiveness. Harry hugged him and asked, "Are you happy now?"

"I am happy to know what you have done for me." Sukhbir nearly cried in his father's arms.

"Come on, son and come on, everyone, we need to be in a celebration mood. Let us first drink and congratulate Sukhbir for his marriage."

Jessica opened the champagne, put it in the glasses for everyone and shouted, "Cheers to Sukhbir's marriage and our wedding!"

Everyone became happy and it was family party time. Jessica wanted to be more romantic and took Karan to the bedroom. Dad and Sukhbir drank a little too much and were a bit drunk. Karan's mum and dad felt shy when they saw Jessica kissing and taking Karen into his bedroom. They wanted to explore if Jessica liked their son. They followed them into Karan's bedroom.

Karan's mother kissed Jessica's hand and asked, "Jessica, do you honestly love my son?" Dad repeated the same question.

"Yes, Mum and Dad, I love your dear boy very much. You don't have to worry." Saying that, Jessica put her arms around Karan and then kissed him.

Mum and Dad smiled and went to their bedroom. It was impossible to see an open expression of love. Mum was taken aback by Jessica's sheer beauty and she expressed her feelings to dad, "Jessica looks like a white fairy. She is a slim and beautiful lady with a perfect smile. She is soft-spoken, so intelligent and will soon be a doctor. Moreover, she is from a respectable family. We are so lucky. What more could we ask for?"

Karan's mum, Surjit, was waiting for her husband's response.

Dad was already fast asleep and snoring loudly.

Jessica After the Truth About Amrita

The following day Jessica brought bed tea to Harwant and Ninder's bedroom. She knocked on the door and said, "Hot bed tea."

Ninder opened the door and Jessica came in with the tray and poured tea into the cups.

"Good morning—did you sleep well?"

"Yes, we had a good sleep. Thanks."

As they sipped her tea, Jessica asked Ninder, "Who is this Amrita—why is she chasing Karen even after marriage?"

"I don't know why she keeps saying that she loves Karan. Rest assured, Jessica, Karan doesn't like her at all," Ninder tried to reassure Jessica.

"Then why did Karan wanted to invite Amrita and her husband to the wedding?" Jessica enquired further.

"I think because they studied together and have always been close friends. Trust me, Jessica, I know my brother-in-law Karan. He would always tell me the truth. He is confused about why Amrita likes him so much. Karan always talks about his love for you. He loves you from the core of his heart. Don't worry about Amrita and don't be so suspicious," Harwant offered more comfort.

"Harwant, you know how she behaves; she sounds like a stalker to me. She could do physical and mental harm to Karen and me. Therefore, Karan should stay away from her," Jessica shared her fears.

"Knowing Amrita, she might appear as an uninvited guest on a wedding day." Ninder was in a naughty mood.

"Shut up, Nindi, shut up!" Harwant got angry with his wife, Ninder, for being irresponsible.

"No, Jessica, she won't come uninvited because she would consider it below her dignity being from the royal family," Harwant reassured.

"My foot, she is from the royal family. She behaves like a commoner. If she does appear, I will throw her out in front of the crowd and not let her spoil my wedding. I am also from a highly respectable and brave family. It will make me happy to throw her out." She picked up the tray and came downstairs half-convinced. She felt a little reassured by Harwant and murmured, "Karan only loves me. He doesn't like Amrita at all."

Wedding Program

They assembled in the lounge that morning to draw the program leading up to the wedding day. Karan's father, Saheb Singh, gave a short lecture about the philosophy behind Sikh traditions and customs.

"Look first; we must include engagement, ladies sangeet with Jago, Vatana and Mehdi ceremonies; Anand Karaj in Gurdwara followed by a big wedding reception. These customs make marriage a very significant event in one's life. Secondly, Laavan during Anand Karaj is the most important to strengthen the relationship between a man and a woman with the grace of God.

"Everyone knows Laavan are wedding verses from the holy book of Guru Granth Saheb. When these verses are read and sung, the couple holding a common piece of long cloth known as Larh goes around the holy book clockwise. The brothers will assist in this circumambulation. Thirdly, Anand Karaj binds the husband and wife together in a permanent bond for the rest of their lives."

"You are right, Saheb. Some other customs we need not perform. I am also of the opinion wedding brings the greatest happiness out of the three main stages of human life, birth, marriage and death," Harjinder Singh agreed with Saheb Singh wholeheartedly.

"I am pleasantly surprised to hear the philosophy behind marriage," Jessica said acceptingly.

"I don't believe in many customs, but if that makes everyone happy, so be it." Karan was happy about the decision his elders made. Jessica had already accepted this and was very much in the wedding mood.

They then charted out itineraries of various ceremonies accordingly. Harry booked the venue for different traditions and he would confirm again. Harry also took the responsibility of securing the religious wedding day at the Gurdwara. Karen and Jessica were assigned to design, get printed and distribute the invitation cards.

From then on started the decoration of the Thames Mansion began. The music centre and guests in the house started playing traditional wedding songs all the time to create a celebratory atmosphere.

"But you haven't decided on our honeymoon," Jessica asked with a laugh.

"That's your job!" Harjinder Singh replied with a sweet laugh.

"Would you like to sing any folklore wedding song, Sukhbir?" Jessica tried to include him in the conversation.

"Normally, the village women would come to the wedding house to sing these songs weeks before the wedding with the beat of a drum called Dholak." Sukhbir was happy to share his knowledge, making him feel important.

After drawing the program, Karan's parents, brother and Ninder came to his bedroom. Karan was anxious because he didn't even have gold rings for engagement or unique bride and groom dresses for wedding ceremonies. Usually, some gold jewellery was also gifted to the groom by the bridegroom's family. His parents had noticed anxiety on his face.

Karan was wondering how he would afford these essential wedding items. His father, mother, brother Harwant and sister-in-law Ninder brought a suitcase. Ninder opened the briefcase and it had in it red boxes with gold rings, bangles, necklaces, earrings, wedding dresses and suites. Mum laid all the items on Karan's bed and opened the boxes. Karan became pleasantly surprised and had a sigh of relief.

"Mum! How and where did you get all these expensive items?"

"Karan, parents know the customs. We kept my jewellery from my wedding. We have already bought some gold for you at your brother's wedding. Ninder also bought some for your wedding. So don't worry. Everything is taken care of," Mum reassured.

"These gold necklaces, earrings, bangles and rings are for your beautiful Jessica, this gold bracelet for your father-in-law, this gold bracelet for their Sukhbir and this gold necklace for your future mother-in-law. Here is the Punjabi wedding dress for Jessica and one for Sarah and Achkan for you and Jessica's dad," Ninder explained in detail.

"But what item of gold is for me?" Karan asked mischievously.

"Jessica!" said Karan's mother lovingly.

"These expensive gold rings with diamond earrings for both of you. These are wedding gifts for you from your brother and sister-in-law." Harwant took the rings out of the box and showed them.

Karan embraced his parents, brother and sister-in-law. Karan became emotional and a few tears rolled down from his eyes on the cheeks. He said in gratitude, "Thank you, my family, you have kept our family's honour."

Engagement and Then Marriage

Preparations for the engagement began the week before the wedding. Harry had confirmed a luxurious venue again, 'Gold Farm' outside London for the engagement and the elegant Park Hotel London for a wedding day.

The decorators have completed the decoration of the Thames Mansion. A large marquee was erected and decorated in the back garden, which could easily accommodate four or five hundred people. Inside is a stage for the bride and groom to sit on a sofa. There was a drinks bar and many decorated round tables and covered chairs.

On the engagement day, only close friends and relatives attended this ceremony. The bride and groom sat on the stage with their parents. The bride's mother put Punjabi sweet laddoo in their mouths and the bridegroom's mother performed the same act. They both then put a ring on each other's fingers. Everyone applauded and the couple came down the stage and started the bhangra dance. Drinks and bhangra dance carried on late at night.

The day before the wedding, the ladies performed the Jago dance. On one side of marquee, all the girls decorated their hands and feet with henna. On the wedding day, the Gurdwara priest performed 'Anand Karaj', also called 'the act for a happy life'. Sikh Guru Amar Das introduced laws which forbid young children's marriage and allow interracial and inter-caste marriages. The wedding ceremony must take place in the Gurdwara.

Before Anand Karaj, the two families meet each other, which is called Milny. First, the father of the boy and the girl met, hugged put garlands of flowers around each other's necks. Because they were old friends, they tried to lift each other in the air but found it challenging. They also exchanged gold rings. Then mothers also hugged and the two put gold necklaces around each other's necks. The brothers met as well and exchanged gifts. It ended with a prayer from a Sikh priest.

After breakfast, they all entered the main hall of the Gurdwara for Anand Karaj. They looked beautiful traditional attires. Both bowed in front of Guru Granth Saheb and sat on the cushioned floor. The religious Sikh hymn singers known as Regis, sang hymns related to marriage in a very melodious voice. The priest requested parents to stand up for prayer called Ardas.

After this, Jessica's dad handed one side of a long silk muffler known as palla to Jessica's giving away his daughter. Regis sang another hymn, "Palle Tende Lagi," meaning I am now yours. Anand Karaj started and after Laavan ended, they were given words of advice by the priest.

The wedding ceremony ended smoothly. Karan and Jessica were now husband and wife. All the guests congratulated the couple and their parents. They both went home to change their wedding dresses for the reception. All the guests reached Park Hotel in their cars and many coaches.

Then there was the grand wedding reception in the Park Hotel in London. In the magnificent foyer, waitpersons served food and drinks to the guests. Then slowly, they were directed by the master of the ceremony to move into a big hall to take seats at their respective round tables.

The florists decorated each table with red roses. There were bottles of single malt, whiskey, Bacardi, vodka and wines on each table. The waitpersons also served a variety of vegetarian and non-vegetarian food. On the stage were big red and gold chairs for the married couple. On one side of the hall, there was another stage on which a Punjabi band played their music.

The married couple arrived outside the hall in a helicopter. Then Karan, Jessica and their families arrived at the hall's door. The Master of Ceremony welcomed them, asked the guests to stand up and gave them a big applause. Sukhbir, Harwant and Karan's friends, Harvey and Bally, were doing the bhangra in front of the married couple with the bhangra group.

The bhangra group was singing and dancing, led to a reserved family table and the couple took their stage seats. The bride and groom looked beautiful in their new outfits. Then dinner was served. The master of the ceremony called the couple to the dancing floor as soon as the dinner was over.

Harwant, Karan and Jessica took turns giving speeches. Karan and Jessica first kissed each other and then danced to their favourite song. Then the Punjabi band started singing Punjabi bhangra songs and everyone joined on the dancing floor. At the same time, the family members and the couple sitting on the guest stage started taking photos of their blessings.

After the function, the couple went home to perform the final ritual known as Pani Varana. Before the couple entered the house, on the doorstep, the mother poured a bit of oil on the sides of the door and then gave Karan a steel glass with water. The groom's mother was asked to drink water from the glass. The bride tried to stop her drinking water. After seven attempts, he let her drink water. They entered the house and rested there for a while.

The newlyweds then drove off to their honeymoon with a large sign pasted at the back of the car.

"Just married!"

Sarah's Changing Behaviour

When Karan and Jessica came from their honeymoon, the house was still full of joy. On the other hand, Karan felt uneasy living with in-laws. His family was temporarily staying there as well.

After the wedding, he could also see a change in Sarah's behaviour towards him and Jessica. Perhaps Sarah was feeling the burden of his family and Sukhbir. He thought the right thing was to discuss this with Jessica. Jessica had also seen a change in her mum's attitude towards her. When Jessica brought breakfast or dinner for Karan in their bedroom, Sarah would funnily look at her and say, "It's all right for some Maharaja to be served meals on his throne. Tell the Maharaja to come down for it."

Jessica empathised with Karan and said, "I never thought my mother would change like that after my marriage so soon."

Sarah could not hide her feeling anymore. One day, Jessica heard her mum arguing with dad. She was saying, "Harry, I don't like too many people in this house. I know you have a lot of fun drinking at the bar daily with your friend! But what about my space?"

"Look, Sarah, they are going back to India soon. Just be calm."

"But what about Jessica and Karan? Where are they going to live?"

"They are our children. They can stay with us if they want." Harry looked surprised at Sarah's behaviour.

"But they are children no more. They are married adults and should live in their own house like any English adults had to do."

"Well, let them become doctors and then I will arrange for them to move."

Jessica shared this argument with Karan. Before the situation escalated, Karan talked to his family and booked seats early for Amritsar. Harry asked Karan to do the same for Sukhbir. Before boarding the plane, Karan hugged his mum, dad, brother and wife. He then hugged Sukhbir. He was in tears and promised, "Mum and dad, when I am a doctor, I will have my own home, then I will bring you back to stay with me as long as you want—and you too, my brother."

"No problem, everything will be fine by God's grace!" Dad and Harwant hugged Karan.

Harjinder Singh, Jessica and Karan felt very disappointed that Karan's family was sent back to India under unpleasant circumstances. Karan felt his family was kicked out of the house. He took solace in thinking that his family was intelligent enough to understand the whole situation..

Sukhbir agreed to go back as well but did not leave happily.

Infidelity

Harry also had a third business partner, Michael Ford, who had one-third of the shares in the company. He was a stakeholder in many other business enterprises. Michael came to London from Ireland and became a prominent property developer by buying and selling small holdings.

Like Harry, he liked his single malt whiskey. They often met in familiar property business places and gradually became friends. They merged their property business and formed a new company 'Angelo-Irish Property Limited Company'. Like Harry, Michael was a brilliant and clever businessman.

Harry has always been busy working in their central London office. Lately, Sarah had started working from home and would only attend board meetings at the office. Karan usually studied in his bedroom because Sarah's attitude seemed to be getting worse daily towards him and Jessica. She would never ask for food or drink. Jessica would make him breakfast and make a sandwich for lunch for him. In the evening, Jessica would usually take him out for dinner.

Generally, in the evening, Sarah would go out, making an excuse that she was seeing her parents or siblings. She would make funny excuses not to sit at the dining table in the evening.

Due to stress at home, Karan was not concentrating on his examination correctly. One night when Sarah was not at home, he asked Harry, "Dad, can me and Jessica move to the flat or any of your properties?"

"Son, I don't want to let you and Jessica go from here. Our community will laugh at me removing you from this big mansion to a flat. Concentrate on your exam and I will find a good house for you. That flat is too small. I will not be able to tolerate my daughter living in a small flat."

"OK, but we can't live in this house anymore," Karan expressed.

Father and daughter looked at each other and felt helpless. They hugged to console each other.

Karan and Jessica decided to stay in the mansion home until Dad found them suitable accommodation.

After being reassured, he ignored Sarah's behaviour and started preparing for the exam. He took the exam but was not sure if he would pass. After the exam, he was supposed to meet Jessica that day but did not feel like doing it.

So, he straightway came home. He arrived home and went upstairs to his bedroom. Karan heard some chaotic noises from Sarah's bedroom. He opened the door and saw Sarah making love with Michael. He quickly shut the door. Sarah was half-dressed in bed linen. She was shouting at Karan. Michael came out half-dressed. Both were nervous and very angry at him, "How dare you open the door of my bedroom?" Sarah shouted at Karan.

Predicting physical abuse, Karan ran down the stairs and took an underground train. He called Jessica, seemed nervous about his exam, "How did your exam go—you seem very nervous."

"Don't worry about my exam. If I fail, I can retake it. It is more serious than that. Wait for me in the red bull pub nearby."

"OK, I will do that," Jessica replied.

They both sat in the corner of the pub lounge. Jessica had already brought him a beer and a gin with tonic. Karan drank a glass of beer.

"Say something, Karan. The exam didn't go well?" Jessica was eager to find out what the matter was.

"I told you it is not the exam. If I fail, I will retake it."

"Then what is it? Tell me soon!"

"I went straight home after the exam and your mum was having sex with that Irishman Michael in her bedroom."

"Are you sure?"

"I saw with my own eyes—one hundred per cent."

"Oh, my God! What have you done, mum?" As if the earth had moved under Jessica's feet.

She couldn't believe that her mum would become so unfaithful and commit infidelity.

"What shall we do now?" Karan was shocked. They tried to calm down and decided they would not go home alone. They would call Dad to pick them up.

"Oh, my God! What will happen to Dad when he finds out his wife has been unfaithful? He already suffers from heart disease." Jessica was terrified.

Jessica called Dad to come early and give them a lift back home. On the way, they dare not tell Dad anything about mum. Dad looked at them nervously and asked, "Son! How was the exam?"

"It was fine, but it was challenging—see what happens?" Karan replied.

Harry encouraged Karan, "Don't worry, you can retake it."

After a short conversation, they remained silent till they arrived home. Sarah had left home. Dad went all over the house and shouted, 'Dear Sarah.' They all went upstairs to Sarah's bedroom. She was not even there. There was dirty, shrivelled linen on her bed and Sarah's wardrobe was empty. All guessed what might have happened. They came to the lounge.

"Looks like Sarah has gone?" Harry didn't seem too surprised, as if he already knew it.

"Dad! I have found this letter Mum has left," said Jessica.

Harry read the letter to everyone.

"Harry! I'm sorry, I'm leaving you. My affair with Michael has been going on for some sometime. Don't chase me. Soon I will send you divorce papers through my solicitor for amicable settlements. I will still miss you and Jessica. Sarah."

Harry threw himself onto the sofa chair with his head leaning backwards. Once again, he became numb. Karan and Jessica were holding and hugging him on both sides but could not say anything.

"Dad, we are very hurt too." Jessica pulled a heart spray out of her dad's pocket and asked, "Dad, have you any heaviness or pain in the chest?"

"No, don't worry, I had already suspected her affair with Michael, but I didn't want to believe it."

Karan went to the bar, brought a brandy shot and gave it to Dad to calm him down. He downed it quickly, took a deep breath and asked for another, "Karan, get me another fill."

Harry swore at Sarah in Punjabi. Then a few tears fell from his eyes. Karan hugged him tightly.

Jessica growled. "Dad! I don't believe Mum will behave like a commoner."

Harry picked up his strength and patted Karen and Jessica. He spoke, "Come on, let's be brave. Thank God you both are still with me."

Company Estate

Harry's morale had improved after a few weeks. It had helped her to live with his daughter and Karan. He loved them so much and looking at them would make him forget all his sorrows. He found it difficult for him to stay at home. The thought of losing his business kept playing on his mind.

Sarah's deception was not easy to forgive. He kept thinking of the reasons why she left him for Michael. He concluded she didn't love him, but she was putting up with him to grab his property. She was a gold digger. He suddenly realised Sarah and Michael were planning to split the partnership in the company behind his back.

He got up from his chair and spoke loudly, "Oh, my God! Both are going to grab my property. After the divorce, Michael and Sarah will take seventy per cent of their shares and I will have only twenty-five per cent. I may have even to let part of my share go to Sarah to keep the house."

Harry started working at their London headquarters to find an amicable partnership solution. He had a long meeting with his accountant and lawyer to discuss the split. Harry informed them about Sarah's and Michael's intentions. He asked them to get a valuation of all the holdings and property.

He also told the lawyer to deal with legal divorce amicably without going to court. The lawyer agreed with this approach. Harry asked them to organise a meeting with his partners to resolve these legal issues without involving him. He could not face Sarah and Michael.

Harry had already registered the property in India in Sukhbir's name well before marrying Sarah. Therefore, Sarah could not claim her share in a property in India. He had not told Jessica and Karan what was happening behind the scenes. Thankfully, after many meetings between lawyers and accountants, they settled the divorce amicably out of court.

After deciding the matter, Harry had twenty-five per cent shares of the total assets. Harry soon realised that with the assets left, he could not afford to live a luxurious life in his mansion in London. He had lots of overhead expenditures.

Therefore, the only choice was to downsize his house and his cars. He wanted to retire because he had had enough of his business and wanted a peaceful life. Luckily, he had accumulated a sizeable private pension he could manage in a small house. He was waiting for Karan and Jessica to start working as doctors.

He put his house on sale without a sale sign-on.

Karan Passed PLAB

Karan thought he didn't do well but passed the PLAB test. At last, there was happy news in the house. Karan wanted to celebrate at home with their friends. After discussing with the dad, they organised a small party around their indoor swimming pool. They decorated the swimming pool for the party.

Karan and Jessica invited their friends, who arrived one by one. Upon entering the swimming pool, the sign flashed, "Well done, Karan, YOU ARE DOCTOR NOW!" The drinks were in ample supply. Waitpersons were serving various types of kebabs and food. DJ started the first English disco songs. Everybody danced, Harvey and Billy began the bhangra dance and the DJ started playing bhangra songs. It was nice to see English and Punjabi mingling and dancing to all songs. Party carried on late at night.

After the party, Karan and Jessica came to the bar lounge, where Harry was enjoying a happy moment with his friends and singing praise for Jessica and Karan. His friends left for us to give time and space to Jessica and Karan with their dad. They hugged Dad and spoke, "Thank you, dad, for organising this party."

"Karan! You are a good doctor and promise me you will never leave my daughter as Sarah has."

"Dad, we love each other so much—this will never happen."

"Promise?"

"Yes, Promise!"

Harry wanted to share happiness with Karan's dad. I'll call your dad, my friend Saheb."

Harry picked up the phone and rang Saheb Singh with a speaker for everyone to hear.

"Hello, dear friend Saheb, congratulations! Karan is now going to be working as a doctor."

"Congratulations to you, Harjinder, as well! I will never forget your big help."

"Well, I will never forget yours as well. Karan is also like my son now. It would be great if you were here today and we would have a lot of fun."

"Yeah, of course. Now all of you should come to Amritsar. We want to re-celebrate the wedding and Karan's success here as well. I am sorry to hear about Sarah, don't worry, life is like that, it brings sorrow and happiness. As you know, these things are sometimes beyond our control. We are always with you. Karan and Jessica will look after you. Just look forward to good days of happiness and try to move on." Saheb Singh showed his empathy.

"Friend! You're right. I can't believe that there are deceitful people in the world. Our religion has taught us to be good human beings, but people around are deceitful."

Jessica was impressed and pleasantly surprised to hear her parents talking about philosophy. They both kept talking on the phone. Exhausted, Karen and Jessica fell asleep and went to their bedroom. But they could hear their dads from downstairs having loud conversations and laughter. Jessica kissed Karan, put on a warm hug and said happily.

"Hello, Dr Karanveer Singh!"

"Hello, my dear would-be Dr Jessica Sandhu!"

Harjinder Singh wanted to share the bad news about selling the mansion with Karan and Jessica, but he restrained himself. He did not want to spoil their happy moments in life.

Jessica Became a Doctor

Harry wanted to move on and be happy. The happy news came when Jessica passed her final medical examination and became a doctor. They all were thrilled.

They attended Jessica's degree ceremony, which was held in the auditorium of University College. The University Staff received all the newly qualified doctors and their accompanying parents or family members in the adjoining hall. They were over-excited and had their professional photos in turn. First, Jessica had her photograph taken in a university robe, hat and replica folded degree. Then the family had a picture together.

The stage secretary called new doctors individually to the stage to receive their degrees. The cameraman took photos while the Dean of the University presented degrees. When it was Jessica's turn, Karan and her dad applauded and everyone else joined in. Then all the new doctors came out of the auditorium very happy, clutching their degrees. They threw their hats together in the air in keeping with tradition. They had a buffet lunch and drinks party with all the doctors and their families.

Harry had already booked a royal suite and dinner for one night at the five-star hotel in London. The suite had a lounge, a private bar and a dining area. The waitpersons came into the lounge and served champagne to them. They cheered Jessica on her success.

"Well done, Dr Jessica! Congratulations!"

Harry had booked room service for a three-course dinner. The waitpersons served the dinner at the beautifully dressed and decorated table and finally brought a cake that read:

"For my sweet daughter, Dr Jessica!"

After the meal, Karan could not help remembering when he, Manav and Amrita received their degrees. But looking at Jessica's happy face, he buried the past quickly. He hugged Jessica tightly, kissed her and said, "Jess, my most beautiful and wonderful wife, I love you."

Harry went to his separately booked bedroom. He wanted to open up to Karan and Jessica about the things that were worrying him, but he did not want to spoil their happiness. He remembered his first wife, Sharanjit. He sighed deeply and dried the tears running down his cheeks; wailing, he said, "Oh, my dear Sharan! Why did you leave so early?"

Move to Leicestershire

Despite the happiness in the family, Harjinder Singh kept reflecting on his loss of business and Sarah. He remained lost and unhappy within himself. He was disappointed because he could no longer afford to keep a big mansion.

He remembered his last day in his office when he handed over his business to Michael and Sarah. He was astonished to find all the staff he had hired for years looked away and were changed dramatically. Michael and Sarah were sitting in the main office celebrating taking over his business with champagne. Before leaving the office, he said goodbye to them for the last time, but they answered rudely.

'Good luck, chap.'

After so many years of partnership, Harry hoped those people would at least give him a good sendoff but seeing their behaviour, he immediately came out and got into his car. He could not tolerate disgusting human behaviour. Harry looked at his business building and felt sick. He vomited in a bag, took a deep breath and came home in a bad state. He went straight to the bar, downed some brandy quickly, splashed water on his face and fell flat on the sofa.

"Oh, my God!" Jessica and Karan rushed to the bar and hugged him.

"What happened, dad?"

"Children! I have lost everything."

"What do you mean, dad, lost everything? Tell us."

Harjinder Singh wiped his eyes and took a deep breath. He was silent for a few moments, held their hands and told them everything. He also told them how badly Michael and Sarah treated him in the office.

"Dad! Don't worry. Everything will be fine," Jessica said lovingly.

"After the business split, we only have this mansion and some cash. I don't want to work anymore at my age. I would not be able to keep this mansion. We will have to sell Thames Mansion," Harjinder Singh opened out to them.

"Dad! We were about to tell you that we both got jobs in Leicester hospitals and had to move. If you want to sell this mansion, we can get an affordable, decent good house in Leicester. Even the big properties are not as pricy as in London," Karan advised.

"Yes, Karan, we have to do something like that. My private pension is enough for daily living. We will have no mortgage in Leicester and we will have no difficulties."

He expressed happiness over this decision, but it was hard to accept downsizing. Harry had already sold his mansion for a reasonable price. They contacted agents and property dealers to find a home in Leicester. They could afford and buy a big house with cash in a Leicestershire village, which was freehold and mortgage-free. Harry made enough profit to lead a comfortable rich lifestyle.

The big house Harry bought in Leicestershire also looked like a small mansion in the suburbs of Leicestershire. In the old days, this house was a watermill over the 'River Soar'.

The previous owners named it Soar Watermill House. It needed a lot of alterations and additional structural changes to convert it into a big house. The house had a few acres of land, beautifully landscaped extensive back gardens on the left side of the river and a long meadow on the right.

The river flew under the large lounge of the house. There were two further large reception rooms, a dining room and a big kitchen. On the left side of the house was a long corridor leading up to a swimming pool with a party area, a jacuzzi, a steam room and a gym.

To the right of the house was a bridge over the river. There was a small old, run-down church on the right side of the river. The dilapidated church building needed a lot of repair work. Harry wanted to convert it into a private Gurdwara, but the council refused, as it was a listed building. Around the church, overgrown bushes and trees were hiding it away.

Harty made the watermill even better by spending more money on internal alterations and decorations. He built a luxurious oval drinks bar and a lounge on the first floor around the old watermill's big wooden wheel. On the first and second floors, there were six large bedrooms with en suites. There were large automatic gates to enter the property. A long drive in front of the house led to a garage for three cars.

The River Soar flew under the big lounge and on the right side of the drive. Harry had a conservatory built to the back of the lounge over the river. It was furnished with Rattan furniture and was a pure comfort zone. From this room, one could observe the flowing river with fish playing and enjoy the natural scenery of landscaped gardens, meadows and a river in the middle.

At the end of the fields, there was an old creaking derelict windmill. The house was smaller than the one in London, but it had a homely feeling. The joy of having a home without debts and no business stress5 Harry was happy living with Jessica and Karan. He had many friends in Leicester and spent many evenings with them in pubs and Indian restaurants.

Naturally, the memory of Richmond's Mansion would sometimes overwhelm him and he would blame himself for not detecting deceit, infidelity and backstabbing. He would then mutter, "What use is to reflect and learn from mistakes after losing everything!"

Amrita's Scary Behaviour

By now, Amrita had become the head of anaesthesia and acute medicine. Manav also became a professor of public health medicine. He had recently become the nodal officer for the Corona pandemic. He had recently eradicated polio from Punjab and had the necessary experience preventing infectious diseases. He is now the Head of the Department of Public Health.

Husband and wife were both fighting to contain the Coronavirus in India. But Manav had a drinking problem and the authorities postponed his suspension because they needed his expertise in controlling the pandemic. Karan was working in the acute COVID ward. Jessica had become head of critical medicine and anaesthesia, looking after COVID patients in ICU. They were also busy fighting Corona in the UK.

During these unprecedented times, Amrita carried on harassing Karan on the phone daily. She did not care whether he was at work or home. Most of the time, he was in awkward situations to answer phone calls. Each time she rang, her rhetoric was how much she loved him and would keep repeating, "I just wanted to be with you. Just ask. I will leave everything here and come to you with open arms."

"Now you are married to him. You should love Manav. He loves you and is not well. Look after him and your daughter, Anamika."

"Manav is very good to me and I understand he loves me so much. He never speaks good or bad about me. But now he has become a complete alcoholic. He is now a secret drinker. I find empty bottles many times hidden in the house. He also has started taking drugs. Anamika was born from a forced bed lock. I wished she was yours."

Amrita had no shame; therefore, Karan would turn off the phone and she would get angry but ring the next day again. Karan informed Jessica of her behaviour and constant phone calls. Jessica felt something very wrong with Amrita, but Karan dismissed it, believing she had just been stupid.

Every time after the phone call, Jessica would insist, "She is constantly harassing you by phoning every day and sending you gifts—she wants you to marry her. This harassment is stalking, which means to get you, she will do anything and may become dangerous to our life."

"No, Jessica! I know Amrita very well. She knew I would never marry her. She wouldn't dare to do any harm to us."

"Well, I shall find out myself. Just pass the phone to me when Amrita rings next time."

When the phone rang again, Jessica grabbed the phone. Jessica was angry with Amrita and told her off in English, "Stop following my husband, you absurd woman. You're supposed to be an honourable doctor from a royal family; you are married to a doctor who needs your help. You should be ashamed of yourself; stop following my husband."

"I know, Didi—you can call me whatever—but we have been friends for a long time. I love to keep teasing Karan by saying, Love you. He only loves you. I will never come into your life except for friendship. I will never call you or him if that makes you happy."

"What do you mean by Didi?"

"It means sister. I do think you are my sister."

"OK. Sister. I didn't want to embarrass you. I understand your friendship is very close. If you want to talk about your old days, I don't mind," claiming Jessica, a sister Amrita seems to win her over.

After this conversation with Amrita, Jessica cooled down. Karan was relieved when Jessica said, "After all, Amrita seems to be a nice lady. She called me sister. But anyway, how could anybody resist a relationship with my handsome husband!"

"You also couldn't resist falling in love with me at first sight," Karan said with a funny smile.

"Sorry, I made a mistake. Your life was more fun in India with your friends. What have you achieved by coming here?" Jessica was a bit playful.

"You! My darling!"

They hugged and kissed each other. Jessica was still sceptical about Amrita's behaviour and indulging in love, she said lovingly, "Listen, Karan. I am convinced she is a jealous stalker. It is also possible she will try to kill me. I think you need to read about the stalkers."

"My dear Jess, we will survive. She wouldn't dare to kill us."

"Now, I will not let you go to India alone," Jessica ordered, putting an armlock around Karen.

"You mean Lockdown Jessica, preventing me from Amrita Virus?" They both laughed.

The following day, over breakfast, Jessica passed an article on stalking to Karan. It read, 'Some people love another person so much that they want them in their life one way or the other. The other person sometimes is not aware of this. Even if he is made aware, he ignores it because he does not love that person. It is one-sided love and such a lover never gives up.

'They harass through the phone, writing anonymous letters and via social media. They send gift after gift. They follow the person to the house and visit quite frequently. These people are known as stalkers. Stalker gives threats to demand love or sex. They will try to develop relationships with other family members to use them to approach the person they love. They make life difficult to live and if, in the end, they are unsuccessful, they do bodily harm and kill the person they love.'

"Stalking is illegal in this country and should be reported to the police." Jessica tried to convince Karan, but he did not take that article seriously.

He again tried to persuade Jessica, "I repeat, my relationship with Amrita has been friendly. She is married to Manav, who loves her deeply and they live happily. I don't think Amrita is a stalker and I am sure she would not harm us."

Jessica couldn't figure out how to explain it anymore. She finally warned him, "Karan, don't you understand she only wants you—She is a clever fox—jealous stalker. If something bad happens, don't blame me for not warning you."

Amrita's More Phone Calls

Amrita kept phoning Karan almost every day. Karan would not pick up her calls most of the time. Now the conversation always started with Manav's health, "Karan, Manav does not stop drinking. He is taking heroin now. He seems tormented by his desire to become a left-wing political leader. As you know, he stood for elections but didn't get elected. He is also becoming jealous of my relationship with you."

"Stop dreaming of your fantasy relationship with me. You should be worried about Manav. Get him admitted to a drug and alcohol rehabilitation hospital." Karan was stern.

"He declines to go to rehab. I am trying very hard to stop him from drinking and taking drugs. He becomes mentally and physically abusive when I ask him to stop drinking. You have to believe I'm doing whatever I can for him." Amrita felt helpless.

"Get her liver tested regularly," advised Karan.

"I had his liver scan done and it shows cirrhosis. His liver is not functioning normally. His performance as a doctor has been risky; therefore, hospital authorities have removed him from the hospital post," Amrita further informed him.

"It may be a good idea if your daughter, Anamika, approaches Manav for rehab and appropriate medical treatment," Karan gave another suggestion.

"Karan, I didn't tell you; she left us to live in London after becoming a doctor. After passing the PLAB test, she is now doing house jobs in London. She hates Manav because of his addictions and our daily arguments. She really likes you," Amrita gave some more information.

"It sounds like Manav will not change. I do not know what else to suggest."

"To make matters worse, he still keeps on going to address unions and when they are on strike, he writes in papers in their favour off them. He is losing weight and he is eating very little."

"Any sign of liver failure?" Karan asked.

"Yes, he has that. He has swollen legs and abdomen and an enlarged liver and spleen. He is becoming forgetful but not confused. His hands shake his stomach and my feeling is if he does not stop drinking, he will die. What should I do? I don't understand. When will you be coming?"

"I am afraid Corona pandemic is not ending and there are travel restrictions and lockdowns. I would not be able to come just yet," Karan expressed his helplessness.

"Alas! I miss you so much nowadays. Every moment I wish you were here. I always have your picture on my mind; I love you so much you can't imagine. I keep yearning for your love," Amrita expressed her intense feelings.

Karan would become nervous when Amrita's talk turned into a lovey-dovey conversation and he would immediately find some excuse to end such a conversation. Then, Amrita would often wonder whether Karan loved her or not. She believed she would get him one way or the other in the end. She kept on making phone calls several times a week and she would end her calls by expressing her love for him and saying, "I love you! I love you so much! My life began with your love and will end with you."

COVID-19 Epidemic in the UK

In the UK, the government convened an emergency cobra meeting in March to draw up a plan to control and contain the Corona epidemic. The prime minister's office at Downing Street daily released government information bulletins for the public on social media such as television channels and radio.

These bulletins gave information on the number and rates of infections, deaths and socioeconomic effects. Also included were new developments and advice on social distancing, wearing masks, improving ventilation, air filtration and quarantine to prevent spread.

The patients' treatments were mainly supportive, but monoclonal antibodies, novel antiviral drugs and doctors started using steroids to improve symptoms. The government had prompted travel restrictions, lockdowns, business closures, quarantines, testing and tracing of contacts of the infected patients and measures to stop the spread of the virus.

The daily death toll rose to more than a thousand in March; by the end of April, the number had dropped. There were instructions to isolate those with a Corona infection for ten days and those who were contacts for two weeks.

By the end of April, around thirty thousand people had died from Corona in the UK. The death toll dropped dramatically in May and June and the government gradually adopted several measures to end the lockdown. People no longer had to confine themselves to houses. They could visit each other. Authorities opened schools, colleges and cinemas, sports centres, restaurants and factories and large shopping centres.

During the pandemic in the UK, another problem arose. Personal protection or equipment, such as gowns and masks, which could have prevented the infection, were in short supply. Sometimes nurses, doctors and other front-line workers were using already used PPE. The government was able to address these shortcomings soon.

Many frontline doctors, predominantly Asian and Black doctors, were prone to this virus and quite a few died. The prevalence of Corona in care homes was also high because they were sent back without Corona tests by the hospital staff and they were also spreading virus infections to the care workers. Because caring staff also worked in other care homes, they also played a significant role in the increased spread of the disease.

Jessica, Karan and their son, Theo, worked in hospitals and battled to treat patients with this viral disease. The health department created new special units called COVID Emergency Medical Units for patients who did not need ventilation. They were moved to the Intensive Care Unit when they required assisted ventilation. All three were on duty in these units, which were full of Corona patients. The admissions were increasing, but even with emergency measures, the hospitals were coping.

Jessica was head of the Intensive Care Unit and was a senior consultant. Her job was to treat more critically ill patients in the Intensive Care Unit (ICU). Many patients were dying and many were kept alive on a ventilator. Each unit has about ten beds which patients always occupy.

With many patients and fewer beds, Jessica often had to make difficult and painful decisions about which patients could be kept or removed from the ventilator. Sometimes she had to work overtime because she was the most senior emergency doctor and was needed most of the time. She did not hesitate at all to do more work.

Like all hard-working nurses, Jessica also had dark mask marks on her face.

COVID at the Watermill House

Working in the hospital's COVID wards, Theo started feeling very tired. One day, he came home with a mild cough and fever. He had tested COVID positive at the hospital and was sent home for quarantine for two weeks. When Theo's dad and mum found out, they got worried. The hospital released Karan and Jessica home for isolation because they were the contacts.

Theo needed isolation in his bedroom. The family took all the precautions to prevent the virus from infecting other members, particularly his granddad Harry. They isolated him in his bedroom. They all received the first COVID vaccine about two weeks ago. They were supposed to have their second dose four weeks later. But the government postponed it to three months after the first dose. Most medical practitioners were not happy with the plan.

Jessica and Karan were both terrified about their son's condition and were checking oxygen saturation and any deterioration in his health. Both were worried and kept comforting each other.

"Let's not worry, He's young and all young patients get better. Nothing will happen to him."

Theo was not getting any better. His parents admitted him to the hospital's high-dependency unit when his condition deteriorated further. X-rays of the lungs showed pneumonia. They were even more alarmed when his oxygen level decreased. He received assisted ventilation. Karan and Jessica wanted to visit their loved one in the hospital, but even though they were working in the same hospital, they could not because of restrictions on visiting.

One night, they cried and felt helpless because they could not be involved in their son's treatment. Anyway, Theo gradually recovered and was discharged home from the hospital.

Harry mainly remained in his bedroom. Jessica would see him from a distance with the mask. The family was using all the precautions to prevent her father from getting infected. They all took extra precautions because their father had had type 2 diabetes, high blood pressure and coronary heart disease. His immune system, therefore, had a low threshold for infections.

After his business had gone bust, he did not care about his health much. He continued to enjoy having a couple of drinks of whiskey a day. Despite all precautions, Harry started having symptoms of Corona and he tested positive. Because of his underlying conditions and being old, his condition deteriorated rapidly. He had difficulty breathing and his oxygen level soon dropped drastically. He was admitted to the hospital ad straightway and needed a ventilator. He had all the standard treatment available at that time.

Again, the family was not able to visit him. Harry deteriorated further and died. Jessica and Karan were very sad and suffered a painful grief reaction. They could not believe it was happening. Theo started blaming himself for Grandpa's death, but his parents reassured him.

"Theo, dear son, you know as a doctor that Coronavirus can transmit itself, even after all the precautions are in place. How it does, it's not fully clear yet. It is not your fault. We also work in a hospital; we could have transmitted it to your grandpa. So don't feel responsible."

Again, sorrow has taken over their life. The saddest thing was their near and dear relatives could not visit them. It is customary in the Punjabi community that all relatives and friends call the deceased home to pay their condolences and console the family. Many were comforting them on the phone and repeating words of Sikh Gurus, "Birth and death are the truth of the cycle of life. One gets liberation or nirvana from this life cycle by coming and going. Harry was a good man who did a great thing in life."

Amrita had heard about Jessica's father's death and she phoned her to show her sympathy, "My dear Sister Jessica, we are both saddened by your dad's demise. Our condolences! We stand by you in your grief. How's Karan taking it?"

Without answering, Jessica passed the phone on to Karan. Amrita said, "I am sorry to hear about your father-in-law's death. It is unfortunate. I do worry about you. Here, Manav wants to talk to you."

"Karan, we are with you in this, friend. We would have come if there were no restrictions." He then passed on the phone to Amrita, who wanted to advise him on cremation rituals.

"Karan, you know all the rituals surrounding cremation. The Sikhs cremate the deceased adults and bury only young children. After cremation, you will have to spread ashes in the

Beas River near Goindwal. As you know, it is customary to first take ashes to Gurdwara for blessing in Govindwal town near Amritsar in Punjab."

"I know all this. I am already organising cremation in Leicester Crematorium and will follow all customs and traditions. I have informed Sukhbir to organise a prayer service at his house in the village. My father-in-law's last wish was to hold his funeral in Leicester, but his ashes to take to Govindwal, anyway."

"If you need any help here, let me know. Is Jessica coming with you? I will wait for you."

"Don't worry; everything is in order. Thanks anyway." Karan put the phone down because the last thing he wanted was Amrita's advice.

Karan planned funeral arrangements with Jessica and Sukhbir. Sukhbir spoke to Jessica on the phone about their dad's demise. They talked about funeral arrangements and they both cried on the phone because they could not be together at their dad's funeral. Jessica cheered him when she informed him she was coming with Karan for final services.

On a funeral day, Karan could invite only close relatives and friends due to restrictions on numbers. Asian funeral directors and the family washed Harry's body in their mortuary. They dressed him in his best three-piece suit. He looked smart with a black tie, turban and black shoes, lying peacefully in a beautiful half-wooden and half-silver coffin.

Asian funeral directors were remarkably familiar with customs and rituals. They brought his coffin home for the last time. A Sikh priest did a brief prayer. They then took the coffin to Gurdwara and the priest again performed prayers.

Finally, the casket arrived in the crematorium, where a few more relatives and friends were seated in the hall. Karan, Jessica and Theo sat in the front seats. Karan, Theo and some relatives picked up the coffin from the car on their shoulders and placed it on a raised automatic platform on the stage. The funeral directors had decorated the casket with flowers and condolence cards. A Sikh religious hymn was playing in the background, chanting, "Wahe Guru, Wahe Guru," means "Wonderful Lord! Wonderful Lord!"

On the left side of the stage, there was a wooden podium with a speaker and a button. This button, on pressing, would take the coffin into the furnace. The funeral service at the crematorium began with the priest reciting specific hymns of life and death called Sohaila from the holy book Guru Granth Saheb.

After the last prayer, named Aardas. Jessica paid tribute to her dad. Then Theo, Karan and Jessica pressed the button together and the coffin slowly disappeared behind curtains. The priest, on behalf of the family, thanked the mourners and informed them, "As you know, the restrictions of holding events, we would not be going to Gurdwara again, which we would normally do for Langar, meaning eating together. On behalf of Harjinder Singh's family, thank you so much for attending his funeral."

The government had eased travel restrictions on flights to India back and forth. The first wave of Corona in the UK was coming under control and the government lifted the lockdown. Thankfully, the Indian Government has also eased some restrictions. Karan and Jessica wanted to fulfil their dad's wish to conduct final prayers at his village and spread his ashes in the river near Goindwal in Punjab. They both took annual leave for a few weeks and decided to go to India. They discussed their plan with Sukhbir and Harwant.

When Amrita came to know their plan, she started ringing Karan, asking for his help for Manav. She kept informing him that Manav's liver was likely to fail soon. He was still drinking alcohol but had cut it down. Manav also rang him for his help and pleaded, "Karan, my days are numbered; I just want to meet you for the last time."

Amrita was very eager to meet him and asked him, "When are you coming?"

"Very soon—I will tell you when we arrive in Amritsar." Karan did not want to invite Amrita to his father-in-law's funeral.

"When—tell me, please. Even if you don't, I have ways and means to find it. Is Jessica coming too?"

"Yeah, she is coming to her father's funeral—shouldn't she?"

"Of course—I wonder how you can find time for me?"

"Could you stop this type of talk in the period of grief? Of course, I will come to see Manav. I will get him to the hospital for appropriate treatment." After saying this, Karan hung up the phone.

As usual, Amrita's phone rang again.

"Why did you hang up?"

"You know it is grieving time for my family," Karan spoke angrily and hurriedly.

"Oh, my God—how is Jessica taking it."

"Badly."

"There is another bad news! I am afraid your parents are not well either. They have tested positive for Corona as well."

"Oh, my God, how are they?"

"I went to see them as soon as Harwant told me. They have a cough and fever and are feeling sluggish a bit. The oxygen saturation level is OK."

"Well, I am going to ring Harwant. Talk to you later." He again hung up.

"Whose phone was it, dad? You look worried?" Theo asked, as did Jessica.

"It was Amrita's phone. She said my mum and dad also have COVID. The test is positive. As Jessica's dad, now my parents. They also suffer from diabetes and blood pressure. If they get pneumonia, they won't survive either."

"Oh my god, now you must go to India soon." Jessica and Theo hugged Karan and tried to comfort him.

Holy City Amritsar

Karan and Jessica arrived at the Amritsar airport. Jessica was born and brought up in England and had never visited Punjab or any other part of India. She had been reluctant to visit India because the media brainwashed her about the poverty in India. She was a second-generation child born to a British mother. Her way of thinking and living was more British. She had learnt little spoken Punjabi but could not read or right.

During the flight, she wanted to know about Amritsar and the Golden Temple and asked Karan about it. Karan told her, "Amritsar, including the whole of Punjab, has a remarkable Sikh history. The airport we will be landing is now known as Sri Guru Ram Das International airport. Recently, airport authorities named after Guru Ram Das, the fourth Sikh Guru and founder of Amritsar.

"The Golden Temple is also known as the Harmandir Saheb, meaning 'Temple of God'. It is the most spiritual and the holiest site of Sikhism. The other holiest sites of Sikhism in West Punjab in Pakistan are Gurdwara Darbar Saheb Kartarpur and Gurdwara Nankana Saheb, the birthplace of Sikhism founder Guru Nanak Dev.

"The fourth Sikh Guru, Guru Ram Das, in the fifteenth century, built this temple with a pool called Sarovar around it.

Our fifth Guru, Guru Arjan, completed Harmandir Saheb and placed our holy book, Guru Granth Saheb, in the sixteenth century. The Gurdwara administration had to repeatedly rebuild this temple for the Sikhs after it became a target of persecution and was destroyed several times by the Mughal Empire. It was also invaded several times by Afghan kings.

"After establishing the Sikh Empire, Maharaja Ranjit Singh rebuilt it in marble and copper in the eighteenth century and encrusted the interior and exterior of Durbar Saheb with gold and worshipers started calling it the 'Golden Temple'. The Golden Temple is an open house of worship for people from all walks of life and faith. It has four entrances and a marble pathway around the pool for circumambulation.

"The four entrances to the Gurdwara symbolise the Sikh belief in equality and people from all castes, religions and races could visit this holy place. The city of Amritsar developed around the Golden Temple. Thus, Amritsar City is now considered a 'Holy City'."

"I understand Sikhs have ten Gurus, the last being Guru Gobind Singh, who broke the tradition of Guruship and named our holy book Guru Granth Saheb as the Guru of all times!"

"Correct, let us go through immigration and collect the luggage. I hope Harwant and Ninder are picking me up from the airport." Karan was in a hurry to get out of the airport.

Harwant phoned them that they were waiting outside and he told him the location.

"Did you bring the ashes; I hope excise and immigration officers do not object to it." Jessica was a bit worried.

"Do not worry before I collect the ashes from the crematorium. I had confirmed that I could fly the ashes to India without any objections," Karan assured her.

After immigration and custom checkup, the public health officers screened for COVID. They showed evidence that they were fully immunised. Still, the officers were adamant about checking for any symptoms. Karan and Jessica introduced themselves as doctors but still performed a lateral test and demanded a fee.

Harwant and his wife Ninder were waiting for him when he arrived at the airport. He was surprised that Amrita was also there to pick them up. Karan and Harwant both hugged and they all greeted each other. Karan then introduced Jessica to Amrita.

Harwant and Ninder hugged Jessica lovingly and expressed their condolences.

"We're sorry to hear that your dad passed away." Ninder's eyes filled with tears and he held Jessica for a long time.

Amrita also received Jessica sobbingly, with love and sorrow, as if she was her sister.

"Harwant! How about Dad and Mum?" Karan asked anxiously.

"They are not well. Both have Covid. As you know, they both were at high risk. They both have pneumonia and tested positive," Harwant told everyone with great sadness and anxiety.

Amrita also could not keep Manav's worsening condition informed, "Karan, I am sorry to inform Manav is also not well. He has not stopped drinking and he does not listen. Against medical advice, he has marched to Delhi with a farmers' protest rally and giving inflammatory speeches."

"Don't worry—let's go home first and then plan what to do," Ninder advised.

"Jessica will ride with me in my car. You all get in your car." Amrita stubbornly put Jessica in her car.

Karan was angry at Amrita and kept saying, "Amrita should not have come to pick us up and Jessica should have declined to ride with her."

"Bhaji, Amrita is your friend, after all. She will make friends with Jessica so she can see you again and again. She pretends to be a very nice lady but can be cunning and calculated. Sometimes we do fear her. She would keep asking me when you were coming. She is so insistent and I had to tell her about you coming," Ninder spoke as usual.

Karan thought it would be nice to keep quiet and not talk about Amrita anymore. He started talking to Harwant about his parents.

"How did they manage to catch Corona?"

"You know, father has this habit of shopping for fresh vegetables from the market. They wouldn't stop going, even during a lockdown. I told them many times to wear the mask, but they would decline. You know how much he loved aubergines," said Harwant.

"I do remember. I used to tease father why he had to buy aubergines?"

Father used to say, "You will know when your bike will automatically take a turn to the market when you grow up."

"I now think because auberges were less expensive compared with other vegetables."

They both laughed at that. Harwant then further informed Karan, "Their condition has deteriorated. I had him admitted to the hospital. I just wanted to tell you about your arrival."

Tears trickle in Harwant's eyes.

"Well, do not worry. We will do what is possible. We shall see our parents soon in the hospital." Karan also became emotional.

Jessica's Encounter with Amrita

Amrita and Jessica sat in the back seat of a chauffeur-driven luxury car. Their car was leading to Amritsar and Harwant followed that car. Amrita wanted to know more about Jessica and she started interviewing her.

"Jessica, I've heard so much about you."

"I hope it was all good!"

"Karan loves you so much. Do you love him?"

"Of course, it was love at first sight. We both fell in love with each other at first sight. I wanted to hug and kiss him when I first saw him, but Mum and Dad were with me so I wouldn't dare."

Jessica told Amrita with great pleasure, remembering that moment.

"What do you think about Karan?" Jessica asked Amrita.

"Very intelligent, lovable and wholly gentlemanly. Why did you ask?" questioned Amrita.

"Just curious about your infatuation towards him." Jessica wanted to explore further.

"Karan has been my friend for a long time; what's wrong with that?" Amrita answered.

"Nothing wrong, but you keep phoning and harassing him," Jessica was confronting.

"That never has been my intention. I keep in touch with Karan for our friendship's sake. Did he ever talk to you about Manav and me?" Amrita asked.

"Oh yes! The three of you are close friends and you like to keep in touch with each other."

"Well, he's such a good friend that I cherish him and worship him as my deity."

"How is your husband, Manav?"

"As you probably know, he is druggy and alcoholic. He has cirrhosis and he is likely to die from it soon. It isn't easy to understand his personality. He loves me and is crazy about me."

"You love Manav?" Jessica asked.

"Not really. I only love Manav because he is my husband. Maybe you don't know our story."

"Karan told me about your whole story that you wanted to marry him, but he did not accept your proposal."

"Is that what he told you—it was a joke—My parents have already arranged my marriage with Manav. I just wanted to make him jealous."

"Did he?"

"I do not know, but after my marriage with Manav, he went to Delhi for an internship and couldn't face us. I then settled with Manav and had a lovely daughter, Anamika, from him. Keeping up with our royal traditions, I have served my husband with mind and soul." Saying this, Amrita felt embarrassed telling lies.

After a few moments, she held Jessica's hand and said, "Sorry."

"Sorry for what—I am not angry with you." Jessica has hidden her suspicion of Amrita's lies.

"I shouldn't have played a joke on Karan with my fake proposal for marriage," Amrita said laughingly.

Jessica could not understand what Amrita was up to and kept quiet until they arrived home. Karan took his luggage to his bedroom and unpacked the bags in the bedroom. It was a strange feeling not to see father and mother at home.

"This house is not so big, but you will like it here," Karan said to Jessica.

"Karan, the house is quite big and spacious and I like its location." Jessica put her arms around Karan and kissed him. After resting for a while, they went downstairs to the lounge. They had tea together. Amrita was still there.

She told Karan, "We have many cars. I'll let you have this new car with a driver while you are here. You go and visit your father and mother. I will make dinner and be ready for you when you return."

Amrita invited herself to stay at their house till late evening. She wanted to be with Karan as long as she could. Manav had gone to the Delhi border to support the Farmers' Protest. Farmers from all over India protested against new laws to bring free marketing to the agriculture industry.

Hospital Visit

Harwant, Jessica and Karan went to see their mother and father. In England, they had advanced experience in managing patients in COVID wards. Jessica had treated these patients who needed intensive care on ventilators. Father and mother were in a private hospital on the outskirts of Amritsar. The Intensive Care Unit, ICU, short of this hospital, like in England, had pretty good standards. Father and mother were taken to the ICU, in case they needed assisted ventilation.

The doctors and nurses there knew Harwant and Karan. Amrita was also the head of that ICU; she was treating them well. They put on complete personal protective equipment, long gowns and head and face cover before they went inside the ICU to see them. Father and mother had some difficulty in breathing. Both observations, such as oxygen concentration and temperature, were within acceptable values.

Karan and Jessica tried to reassure his father, "Dad, you are being looked after very well. Amrita is aware of your condition. Jessica also has a lot of experience in looking after. We are all here and will get you out of the hospital soon."

"Karan—Jessica! Please save us." Father was crying and begging for more help.

Karan was devastated to see them like this. His eyes filled with tears. Jessica consoled him, "Don't worry; father and mother are on the right treatment and if breathing gets worse, then Amrita had planned to attach them to a ventilator."

Karan wanted to hug his parents, but he had to keep his distance. They could not stay there long. They both came out and informed Harwant about their parent's condition and he felt like crying but kept calm. Jessica presented her opinion, "Karan, Harwant, the condition is not that serious, but as we know, their conditions can worsen. On the other hand, God willing, they might pull through."

They were all anxious and frightened due to the uncertainty of the situation. As doctors faced, this uncertainty was routine and with their skills, they could manage uncertainty very well. Corona was a novel virus with no cure available, creating frightening uncertainty.

On the way home, both brothers kept telling Jessica, "Our father was our power of intelligence and mother was strength. We must be brave and realistic. We must prepare and realise that they may die."

Karan kept mentioning what his father said before they came out of the ICU, "Karan! save us—I made you a doctor, save us—please do something, do something!"

They came home very sad and anxious. No matter how brave they were, the Corona pandemic frightened them. Seeing a picture of father and mother in the lounge, Karan bowed his head to their photo and then that of Guru Nanak Dev and prayed with two hands together, "Dear God, save our father and mother from Coronavirus, which has already taken many lives, including my father-in-law. Have mercy on humanity!"

Harwant came into the lounge.

"Come on in the dining room and dinner is ready."

"Can we first have a quick shower and freshen up? I need a couple of scotch before dinner."

"OK, hurry up. I will prepare drinks." Harwant also needed a couple of drinks.

When they came down, Harwant, as usual, measured the double shots of whiskey. He made gin and tonic for Jessica. Jessica also asked Ninder and Amrita for a drink. They didn't drink alcohol and had soft drinks. They felt relaxed a bit and to conceal their anxiety, they started cracking jokes about Corona and the lockdown.

"I'll tell you a Coronavirus joke now, but you'll have to wait two weeks to see if you got it!

"Two grandmothers were bragging about their precious darlings. One of them says to the other, 'I am so good at social distancing, they won't even call me!'

"Did you hear the Coronavirus joke? Never mind, I don't want to spread it around!"

"My mum always told me I wouldn't accomplish anything by lying in bed all day. But look at me now! I'm saving the world!

"What did the sick parent make their kids for lunch? Mac and sneeze!

"What's the best way to avoid touching your face? A glass of wine in each hand!"

"What should you do if you don't understand a Coronavirus joke? Be patient!"

"Enough of jokes; dinner is getting cold," Ninder announced.

"I prepare the food; Karan will love it," Amrita pronounced.

"What have you made?" Jessica asked with curiosity.

"Mahan Mothan Dal and mutton chops—these are Karan's favourite dishes," Amrita said casually.

"Amrita, you seem to know Karan's tastes as well." Jessica was a little jealous.

"I also know what label clothes and perfume he wears."

"How did you know that?"

"As I said before, we have been friends for a long time and during my medical college days, I used to do the shopping for Manav and Karan. You know, Manav never liked any brands. Manav, being a socialist, doesn't believe in labels. I loved the way Karan looked in his clothes."

"Really?" Jessica was somewhat taken aback by how Amrita kept going about her husband.

"Forget about Karan; my husband Harwant looks smart in any clothes. Let's not forget eating," said Ninder to prevent Jessica from further harassment.

Before Amrita went home, she announced, "If you don't mind, I will be around daily."

The Ritual of Spreading Ashes

After Amrita had gone, they decided to go to Goindwal to spread ashes the following day. This Punjab ritual is known as 'Asat Tarna', which involves pouring ashes into the Beas River near Goindwal.

After the Asat Tarna ceremony, everyone planned to go straight to the village. To fulfil the last wishes of Harjinder Singh, Sukhbir had already organised a prayer service in his village. Harwant and Ninder were going to return to Amritsar to be around their sick parents in the hospital.

The following day, Sukhbir came. He wanted to hug Jessica and cry, but they stayed away from each other and mourned from a distance. While expressing his grief, Sukhbir started crying and Jessica began to sob. Karan kept his emotions under control and tried to console them both.

"Be brave, your dad was a great man and he always wanted to see the happiness on his children's faces. Let's celebrate his achievements and say goodbye to his soul happily."

After breakfast, they arrived at Goindwal in cars with ashes. They first bowed in front of Gurdwara Goindwal Saheb. Then Sukhbir went down a tunnel with eighty-four steps leading to an underground lake of holy water known as

Amrit or nectar. The name of this tunnel was Bolly Saheb. Sukhbir brought Amrit water in a plastic bottle. They washed the bottle filled with ashes while chanting Sat Naam, meaning God's Name is Truth.

According to the custom, Sikhs wash the bones or Asats of the dead body with this holy water, but people from foreign countries only bring ashes left over after cremation. After this ritual, they took the ashes to the banks of the Beas River, about two miles away, where they performed the Asat Tarna custom.

When they arrived at the river site, they were surprised to see Amrita was already wearing a white robe customary for that occasion. According to Indian custom, all wore white garments. Jessica had previously wanted to wear a black suit according to European tradition, but Ninder told her to wear a white Punjabi suit with a white head covering.

Next, Amrita autocratically took charge of the rest of the ceremony. It was not a time for arguments and they let her take control of the rest of the ritual. She led them to a unique balcony on the bank of the Beas River. She grabbed the ashes bottle from Karan and placed it on Jessica and Sukhbir's hands. Then Amrita chanted Sat Naam Waheguru and told them to pour the ashes over the river water.

Then they all sat on the bank of the river in a small Gurdwara and the priest read some verses from the holly book and then prayed for Harjinder Singh to rest in peace. Jessica expressed her wish to go back to Goindwal Saheb Gurdwara and climb down the eighty-four steps of Baoli Saheb.

On the way back, she requested Sukhbir to enlighten her more about Goindwal Saheb and Sukhbir responded with great pleasure, "Goindwal town is also popularly known as

Goindwal Saheb. As you know, ten Sikh Gurus were e the spiritual masters of Sikhism. Our first Guru Nanak Dev founded the Sikh religion in the fourteenth century. This town was founded in the sixteenth century by Guru Amar Das, the third Guru of the Sikhs. The major road from Lahore to Delhi used to pass through this town.

"Due to its proximity to the Beas River, Goindwal became a business centre. A businessman or merchant named Govinda saw the potential for this place to become a business centre. He approached the second Sikh Guru, Angad Dev, to establish a town there. He took the Guru's blessing to establish the town. Our third Guru, Amar Das, a disciple of Guru Angad Dev at that time, took over this project.

"After the town's establishment, it was renamed Goindwal after the merchant Govinda. Guru Amar Das settled in this town forever. While living in this city, Guru Amar Das had a slanting well dug in the ground with eighty-four steps to reach the water level. This well-supplied water to the workers and inhabitants of the city. It was easy for people to fetch water through the stairs in the well. The life of Guru Amar Das is engraved on the round roof above the stairs.

"Gradually, people started considering this a religious place; its water was considered holy and called Amrit or nectar. This well was named Baoli Saheb. Japji Saheb is the Divine Word revealed to Guru Nanak Dev by God. Sikhs believe that reciting the Divine Word at each of the eighty-four steps and taking a bath in the water Baoli provides Moksha, liberation from life cycles.

"Apart from this step-well, there is Goindwal Saheb Gurdwara and a big dining hall where Guru Amar Das first started Langar, meaning eating together. The free food is served in Langar in each Sikh Gurdwara in the world and people of all faith can access it. In Goindwal Saheb, Guru Amar Das wrote seven thousand and five hundred lines of holy verses known as Bani in poetry form. He wrote another Bani 'Anand Saheb'.

"The fifth Guru, Arjun Dev, incorporated his hymns into the Sikh scripture, 'Guru Granth Saheb'. Through his hymns, Guru preached the equality of women like Guru Nanak Dev and denounced the ritual of Sati. In this ritual, when the husbands died, their widows had to burn themselves to death by jumping into the burning pyre of their husbands. The Guru also ended this horrible ritual and said that widows could remarry. Here is the history of this holy place."

"Well done, Sukhbir, I didn't even know that," Karan was amazed at his knowledge.

"Bhaji, I have read all the Sikh history. Much of this was in our syllabus in school before doing my degree," said Sukhbir proudly.

"Oh my gosh, Sati must be the horrible ritual for women then! Guru Ji did great work to put a stop to this." Jessica was saddened to know the history of women but also happy to know the great deeds of her Gurus.

They arrived again at Goindwal Saheb Gurdwara. All had head and face covering. First, they started descending the stairs of Baoli Saheb. Amrita grabbed Karan's hand to steady herself. Jessica looked at Karan with her disapproval and Karan understood. He released his hand, pretending to slip and held Jessica's hand to please her, but she declined.

They did not have a traditional dip in the holy water but sprinkled it on their forehead and slowly climbed the stairs. All except Jessica recited Japji Saheb while taking steps upwards. Amrita asked them to sit inside the Gurdwara and listen to spiritual utterances from the holy book known in Punjabi, 'Banni'. After listening to the Banni for a while, they went to eat Langar.

After completing the Asat Taran ceremony, they returned home worrying about their father and mother.

Deterioration of Parents' Health

Karan's parents' condition was not improving. They went straight to the hospital with Jessica, Amrita and Harwant. Father and mother now had low oxygen levels. Suddenly there was a high demand for oxygen cylinders even in that private hospital in Amritsar. Harwant rang around different hospitals and friends and bought cylinders for his parents for a very high cost. His parents then had a high concentration of oxygen delivered by a positive pressure machine. Their condition slightly improved.

Corona was spreading again in cities like Delhi, Maharashtra and Kerala. There was a shortage of oxygen supply due to high demand all over India. Deaths also began to occur due to a lack of oxygen. There were up to four or five thousand deaths every day. The government did not plan well to stop the second wave of the covid. There was a severe shortage of oxygen and hospital beds all over India. Gurdwaras started offering oxygen free of charge, called 'oxygen Langar'.

Due to the increased deaths, there were long queues for funerals in the crematoriums. Firewood for cremation was in short supply; therefore, people were throwing dead bodies in rivers. People were praying to seek God's help. Still, the death toll in Punjab remained very low. The first dose of Covaxin was given to all doctors, nurses, other health workers and older people. Karan's parents were also vaccinated two weeks back. When their parents' condition became stable, they came home and decided to go to Harjinder Singh/s village to perform final prayers.

Final Prayers

Sukhbir had already planned for a small final service for his father in his house. The custom was to recite the holy book by the priest for seven days, leading to the last prayer on the third day. Sukhbir came to the village the same day after the Goindwal ceremony.

Karan decided to go there with his family on the day of the final prayers. But Jessica was in a hurry to see her dad's village and his farm. While they were making travelling arrangements for Jessica, Amrita arrived and offered her services, "Karen, leave that to me. Jessica can come with me in my car."

"No, no need for her to go with you—you should be looking after Manav. I want you to be with my parents, who may need a ventilator in your ICU," Karan urged Amrita.

"Don't worry. I've made all the arrangements for their care. Manav is still on the Delhi border supporting the farmers' protest."

Jessica liked the idea of going with Amrita because she also wanted to know more about Amrita's relationship with Karan.

The next day was the final prayer, also known as the bhog of Harjinder Singh. During the ceremony, the village councillors paid homage to Harjinder Singh one by one. All guests then ate in the Langar. Sukhbir and Jessica had already made all the arrangements to avoid COVID infecting guests.

Harjinder Singh had built a big house with a farm around it, large hall, lounge, kitchen and five bedrooms with washrooms. He has kept one big bedroom for his holidays. Jessica used that bedroom.

After the service, Jessica and Karan went to the bedroom. Jessica hugged Karan to express her sorrow, remembered her dad and could not help sobbing on his shoulders. Being in Karan's lap, her sadness slowly transformed into sweet love and they lay down on the bed. They loved each other and fell asleep. After a while, Jessica opened her eyes, looking very sweet and beautiful; she woke Karan up. She looked sharply into eyes, "Karan! Do you love me?"

"Any doubt?"

"Yes—Amrita has created doubt in my mind."

"What was she telling you?"

"When we came to the village from Amritsar, she kept praising you; she was openly expressing her love for you. She claimed that you, Karan, couldn't live without her. You used to call her secretly and you often visited her whenever you were in Amritsar. She also claims that you only love her and no one else. Is this true?"

"Oh, my God! You believed in her lies. I have often told you she is mad and suffering from one-sided love syndrome. She is a crazy woman. When we were young and naive, we swore that we would help each other in times of hardship. I swear if I've ever loved anyone, it's only you, Jessica. You know I fell in love with you the first sight. She probably is jealous of you; please take no notice of what she says."

Jessica smiled a little and kissed Karan.

"Let me warn you, my dear husband—stay away from her—I repeat, her behaviour is just like a stalker—stop meeting her. She may cause harm to me or you. Thank God she decided to go to Delhi to look after her husband," Jessica once again tried to convince Karan.

"I wouldn't let her harm us. Don't worry." Karan was protective.

"Anyway, how are father and mother?" Jessica asked.

"Stable, but I have no idea what was going to happen to them." Karan was anxious.

"I am happy to see my dad's house and farm in the village," Jessica said joyfully.

Karan shared her joy, but then he had news for Jessica, "I have good and bad news for you."

Good and Bad News

"Which news do you want to hear first, good or bad?" Karan asked Jessica.

"Of course, good one first."

"The good news is that Sukhbir got married to that beautiful maid, Raj. He did not let anybody know about him getting married. He told me about our wedding in England. He was afraid your dad wouldn't let him marry a girl from a very low caste. She is our new bride now, living in this house."

"Really? That's a real surprise. If it is a love marriage, it is marvellous. I wholeheartedly support them. I will now pamper our bride correctly and we will accept her into our family. Oh, I am so happy for Sukhbir. What is the bad news?"

"Not so bad. Sukhbir asked if dad had officially registered this farm and house in his name. If I tell you, I hope you will have no objection. Before your dad died, he gave me the legal registry of this property in Sukhbir's name. I brought it because I knew Sukhbir would ask for this."

"I have no objection. Dad has done the right thing. The property here will be his wedding present. He will now feel delighted that dad has done this for him. It is good news, not a bad one."

Getting out of bed, he pulled her dad's will and registry papers out of his bag and handed these to Jessica. Karan was worried that Jessica would get upset after knowing this.

There was a knock on the bedroom door. Karan asked to come inside. Sukhbir's wife, Raj, came in and said, "Bhaji, sister, the food is ready; it's on the table—let's eat!"

Raj was a beautiful lady with blue eyes and white colour. She belonged to a lower-caste family. The landowners kept such girls in their households for cleaning and daily chores at home and farm. If Harjinder Singh had known, he would not have allowed this marriage to happen.

"Raj, come here to me!" Jessica asked her to sit beside her.

"Yes, sister"—embarrassed she came to her.

"Congratulations on your wedding."

"Thank you."

"Do you love Sukhbir?"

"Yes, very much so," she said and then got embarrassed.

Raj ran downstairs into the kitchen. She had laid food on the dinner table. Jessica and Karan followed her. Before they started eating dinner, Jessica handed over the will and registry papers to Sukhbir and said, "This is your wedding gift from your dad, whom you called Burha. Congratulations!"

Sukhbir had a quick look at the deeds. He became emotional and said, "I can't thank you enough, dad; you have made me happy. I can now be proud of you. I'm not alone anymore. I now have the farm and this house in my name; I got my sister, brother and Raj; we are family, after all."

"There is one thing, though, would you let us stay on the farm if ever we visit you?" Jessica asked.

"This is our dad's property; you can stay with us any time. Dad's room now is yours." Sukhbir showed brotherly love.

Then the family had their dinner. Before they went to their bedrooms, Amrita rang, "Manav's condition has deteriorated and she is in the ICU in Delhi. He is begging for Karan to come and help him medically."

Lying in bed, Jessica was staring at the ceiling, but the clouds of anxiety were thickening in her mind. She was anxious to return to her ICU at his hospital in England. Then she feared Karan would not stop going to Delhi. She was worried that Karan's parents might not be able to survive.

She also feared another 'Corona variant Amrita', who she felt was more deadly than COVID.

Manav; Victim of COVID

While marching to the red fort in Delhi in a farmers' protest, Manav collapsed. Ambulance paramedics took him to a liver hospital in Delhi, where he had a positive COVID test. Amrita had to go to Delhi, leaving Jessica in the village. They watched Manav marching and then collapsing on television. He had not stopped drinking even while staying with farmers in protest camps. Karan got another phone call that he was deteriorating.

"Oh, my God!—one trouble after another. I'm sick and tired of bad news. God bless and protect everyone." Karan had never sought God's help before.

"I have to see Manav probably for the last time. I don't think he will survive."

"I might come with you as well."

"We will see him and go back to Amritsar—and then back to England."

Manav had underlying liver failure and low immunity to COVID. Karan was angry that Manav, even a doctor, did not care for himself and that Amrita may have deliberately stopped looking after him from drinking alcohol. He also realised that Jessica didn't like his relationship with Amrita and she seemed right in thinking that Amrita might be a stalker.

"What are you thinking?" Jessica asked.

"I think you are right; Amrita could be a stalker and will do some harm to us."

"Then we shouldn't go to Delhi to see your friend. Amrita is a doctor and perfectly capable of looking after her husband," Jessica pleaded.

"I understand, but the problem is she purposely neglects him and doesn't look after him. She says if he wants to commit suicide by drinking, let him do it. I think she is deliberately doing this."

"Then why do you have to care? I don't understand this kind of friendship and this we have never seen in the western world. You also told me COVID is spreading in Delhi."

"I do understand, dear! I feel strongly about seeing him before he dies. After seeing Manav, I promise I will break all ties with Amrita."

"Well, you should be more concerned about your parents."

"We will see him tomorrow and take an evening flight to Amritsar."

They arrived in Delhi the next day via plane. They went to the hospital to see Manav. Amrita had been waiting in the reception. Taking the elevator, they went up to the third floor. Amrita introduced them to Dr Verma, a liver specialist and then they went to the liver ward. Dr Verma discussed Manav's condition and told them the prognosis for survival was poor. He now has liver failure due to cirrhosis.

Looking at them, Dr Verma further informed me, "At present, he is stable but a little confused. He has not developed

Covid related pneumonia yet. The lungs are still working and oxygen saturation is still fine. He has oxygen and other standard medicines, but no ventilator is needed. This morning I performed upper endoscopy on him, which showed dilated veins in the lower part of the gullet, which may rupture at any time. I have put a band around these to prevent bleeding, but I also found several extended veins in the stomach. Let's go and see the patient."

They went inside Manav's room and he was not fully conscious. He was drinking carrot soup.

"Manav recognised me?" Karan asked.

"Karan, of course, I recognise you. I am OK. Take me home, please. Come on."

"No, you're not going anywhere until you completely get better."

"It seems Corona will kill me and the whole world."

"Don't worry; you will get better with the treatment," Jessica introduced herself.

"Jessica, I wish I had met you in the right state of mind. Thanks for marrying and looking after my friend Karan. He deserved the most beautiful and intelligent girl like you. If I recover, I will give up drugs and alcohol forever and arrange a grand reception party for you. I was hoping you could take me home to Amritsar. We are all doctors and we know the only treatment for my illness is glucose and carrot soup. Surely, you can treat me at home," Manav muttered, taking another sip of the soup.

"You also have COVID, which may lead to pneumonia and you may need a ventilator. That's why it's not appropriate to go home," said Amrita.

But Manav was annoyed by Amrita's advice. He took a long sip of the soup and said, "I will not stay here. Just take me home."

Annoyed, he immediately started coughing and vomiting blood mixed with the soup. Then he heaved and started bringing up a lot of pure blood from his mouth. Manav fainted and his heart stopped.

Amrita ordered an emergency team and a trolley. Amrita began to resuscitate him with chest strokes. Jessica inserted a tube into his windpipe and started giving oxygen through it. But Karan's heartbeat started fibrillating. He had several electric shocks. His heartbeat completely disappeared on the heart monitor. Attempts to revive him failed.

All decided to declare him dead.

Manav said goodbye forever. Amrita clanged to Karan tightly and she started crying loudly. Jessica, showing sympathy, slowly separated them and hugged Amrita to console her. She kept crying and calling Manav to come back. Karan also had tears rolling down his cheeks. Dr Verma asked everyone to go to the staff room so that they could proceed with looking after the dead body. The porters wrapped Manav's dead body in a plastic bag and zipped it over.

Amrita was still crying and informed Manav's dad of his son's death. She then called her daughter in London to tell her dad's passing away. Both were crying on the phone for a long time. Anamika could not attend his father's funeral because of another local lockdown in London.

Dr Verma again expressed his sorrow and helplessness, saying, "Sorry we all could not save Dr Manav. As a doctor, you know that he had very little chance of survival from COVID with underlying liver failure."

"Doctor, we knew that. Thank you for trying to save him," Amrita replied in sorrow.

"We will perform Manav's funeral at Amritsar. Manav's dad would also want it in Amritsar. He is on his way here and we will take Manav to Amritsar in the car. There are long queues of dead people from COVID waiting at the crematorium here in Delhi," Amrita informed.

"Well, if your father-in-law is coming, we should go to Amritsar. You know he doesn't like me. He always accused me of making Manav an alcoholic and drug addict while I tried to get him off drugs and alcohol. If he sees me here, he will accuse me of Manav's death," Karan reminded Amrita.

"There is no time to go into such things. I have explained your innocence to my father-in-law many times. You go to Amritsar and if you can, please make arrangements for a cremation," Amrita instructed Karan.

Karan and Jessica took a flight from Delhi to Amritsar. Jessica was still amazed at Karan's close friendship. She had never seen such a friendship in Europe with so much love, care and brotherhood. During the flight, she kept talking to Karan about their weird company.

"This friendship is like you are married to each other."

"Jessica, we are not married, just good friends. Friendship includes affection, love, harmony, compassion, devotion, honesty, selfless service, loyalty, mutual understanding and kindness," Karan gave a brief lecture on friendship and Jessica.

"OK, Professor, I don't need a lecture. Let me join your friendship triangle. I may find your love for me too." Jessica nodded.

"You are my only love, Jess; my wife, my life and everything." Karan kissed Jessica's forehead lovingly and took her in his arms.

"Karan, on what grounds Manav's father blames you for his son's addiction?" Jessica wanted to know.

"He is a very awkward, retired military man who dislikes people of other castes. All three of us were always toppers in every class, but my results were better than Manav and he became jealous. He wanted me not to meet Manav, but he could not stop him from meeting me.

"During medical college, Manav started drinking and taking drugs. He befriended those students who believed in bringing a revolution in India through extremism. But could not do anything. He continued taking alcohol and drugs after marriage to Amrita. Rather than encouraging, I have been trying to stop him from taking alcohol and drugs," Karan told his story.

"I understand; let's not talk about it and leave it as that. Let me know the friendship amongst our dads," Jessica instructed.

"Jessica! Our parents' friendship was classical, as I have defined friendship before. Your father did not own much land then; my father was a businessman. Despite belonging to different castes, they were good friends. Your father was not earning much money from the land and he expressed his wish to come to the UK.

"My father helped him with airfare and took three dollars. With this help, he came to the UK and worked hard. Before your dad became a property dealer, they had an import and export business in hosiery manufacturing. Your father probably would not have allowed me to marry you if they had not been friends."

"It's nice to know they were good friends, accommodating to each other. We should always be proud of their achievement," said Jessica.

"They were perfect friends, helping each other in friendship," Karan said on landing.

Back Home in Amritsar

On arriving home in Amritsar, the two brothers were happy together. They both like to discuss their worries and gain the confidence and courage to deal with current situations. Ninder went to the kitchen to cook and Jessica followed her and said to Ninder, "I would like to cook English food today. What can we do?"

"We have an electric oven—I could roast chicken. Let's get the chips out."

"OK—we like chips. I roast some potatoes and make gravy?"

"Yeah, all sounds fine to me."

"You make a gin and a tonic for me, Harwant and I do the roast."

Ninder and Jessica were cooking and laughing. After Manav's death, Jessica informed Ninder of Amrita's behaviour, "Ninder, I cannot understand Amrita, do you?"

"As I told you, she is supposed to be a princess. She is a great-granddaughter of a local Maharaja or a king. Her parents own a colossal palace not far from here. Manav also lives with them. Amrita's parents raised her like a princess, but she loved our family so much that she considered her father and mother as her parents. She also knows Sukhbir and his love affair. She often says, "I wish! I can be the daughter-in-law of this house."

"What do you mean?"

"Wedded in our family."

Busy talking, they burned all the food in the oven and filled the house with smoke. They opened all the doors and windows. Harwant ordered home delivery for food.

After dinner, they went to their rooms but were worried about their parents. They buried their heads in the pillows and tried to sleep. The fear of COVID deaths kept coming into their nightmares in one form or the other. They had a restless night of sleep and kept getting up. They woke up in the morning worried about their father and mother. Harwant had to go to his hospital and was on duty all day. He didn't have much time to see his parents.

While having a quick breakfast, he murmured, "What is the point of becoming doctors in our family if, in the end, we cannot save parents and patients from this pandemic? I do not think our parents would survive either. What's the point of being a doctor?"

Everyone was looking at Karan to answer, as he was the first doctor in this family. Karan spoke with empathy but loudly and clearly, "As doctors, we are trained to save people from diseases. That is why we have become doctors. I am very proud to be a doctor saving lives. For me, there is no better profession."

Jessica heard him and said, "And we are not gods. If, after doing our utmost best but patients die, we should know that this is the doctor's life. The COVID vaccine and other measures will soon beat this pandemic. We must win this war; let's keep our strength and courage to do so."

Manav's Funeral

Amrita and her father-in-law arrived home with Manav's body. She looked at Manav's face and remembered the good days with him. She felt sorry for him for not making it to be the leader of his party. She felt sorry for his ambition to revolutionise India for the better. She touched his face and felt his stiff body in Rigor Mortis and said sobbingly, "Manav, you will come back in your next life as a top leader!"

There was no place available for Manav's funeral in Amritsar cremation. His father decided to cremate his son in his village cremation. The next day, they took his body to the village. Many villagers gathered in front of their houses to protest this cremation. They were misinformed that the dead would spread COVID in the village.

Karan confronted them and explained that the dead body would not spread the virus. He also informed that they followed the Public Health Department's instructions to prevent the Corona spreading. The villagers accepted this grudgingly and dispersed.

Manav was cremated in the village crematorium according to Sikh traditions and customs. While the pyre was burning, Karan sat down on the top of an old well nearby and remembered how Manav once tried to kill himself after getting drunk by jumping into that well. Karan wanted to prevent him from taking such drastic action. He had argued with his father earlier.

After the argument, Manav jumped into the well and got stuck in the mud in shallow water. Manav tried to free himself but was unsuccessful. His father tried to stop him, but he could not.

"Save Manav, Karan," Major asked Karan in panic.

All workers came around, but no one dared to down the well. Karan climbed down on the water wheel by using its baskets as steps. He grabbed Manav's arms and shouted, "Turn the wheel anticlockwise to pull him out."

It worked and he brought Manav out of the well and everyone clapped.

While he remembered that Jessica was talking to Manav's father, Jessica told the Major that it was not Karan's fault that Manav got into addiction. On the contrary, he has always tried to stop him from doing that because they were best friends. Amrita again confirmed what Jessica had said. Manav's father, after listening and remembering how Karen saved Manav from the well.

He realised that he was hard on Karan, started sobbing and apologised, "Karan, I am very sorry for how I have been treating you. I was jealous and angry at Manav for not getting more marks than you. Sorry, I took my anger out on you and called you unworthy of becoming a doctor. Our community knows that Karan and his family are the pride of this village. Your father, being a businessman, helped the villagers financially. He had also helped me financially."

"Why are you still looking at in the well?" Manav's father asked Karan.

"I see Manav standing in the mud, with his raised arms like a revolutionary leader. Come on, soldier, we will bring the change for the best in our country."

"Karan, I hope you will forgive me. I know you have tried many times to save my Manav. I behaved in bad ways. I heard you and Jessica are doing well in England. I wish you could come back because we need you here," Major said emotionally.

After the cremation, they went to Major's house. They had tea, a Karan asked permission to leave. Jessica expressed her desire to see Karan's old house in the village where he was born. They quickly visited his old house on the other side of the village. It was empty and in a derelict state.

Jessica was pleased to meet Karan's cousin, who had built his beautiful house nearby and was looking after family properties. They went to his house and were surprised to see Amrita was already there. She had visited Karan's old house many times and knew Karan's cousin and family well.

"I have come here so that you don't leave me behind. I have also decided to go back to Amritsar," said Amrita.

After the meal, they all arrived home at Amritsar. They sat in the lounge and all were very sad. Amrita also sat on the couch nearby. Karan was surprised at Amrita and told her, "You should have stayed with the Major until the final prayers."

"I'm worried about your mum and dad too—now Manav's funeral is over, I had to return to my ICU. I will be coming here frequently if you don't mind; I want to spend more time with you before you return to England. Anyway, I need your psychological support after losing my husband."

Saying that, she started crying and again reached out for Karan's hug. Jessica instructed by shaking her head to stay away. This instruction made Amrita very annoyed and she cried even more. When she stopped crying, everyone went to the dining room to have dinner. Amrita invited herself to the dining table.

At the dinner table, Amrita started crying again and said, "I have no one left apart from my parents. I don't even have my daughter around me. I consider you as my family. Before leaving, at least for the sake of my friendship, at least have dinner at my house tomorrow evening. Also, my parents want to see you."

Jessica's eyebrows furrowed, listening to Amrita's invitation.

After dinner, Amrita went to her home. Jessica was still angry and said, "Why doesn't she leave us alone?"

"Friends are friends—and many use friendship to be with their lovers too. Amrita is very upset and grieving. She considers us as her family. We should at least be sympathetic towards her; after all, she is a Royal Lady," Ninder said sarcastically.

Jessica held Ninder's arm and took her to the bedroom and closed the door and said, "My Foot Royal Lady! Ninder, you're mistaken. She is not a nice lady but a 'paranoid' stalker."

"We should try to keep that lady at arm's length; otherwise, she will do some harm to us."

Karan followed them and tried to explain to Jessica.

"I think she wants our sympathy and support after her husband's death because of our old friendship. All her life, she has been struggling to live with Manav."

"But Jessica's point also sounds right. She is paranoid about Karan. She wants to keep her relationship going with our family to keep meeting him. She used to visit us with Manav only to learn about Karan and his family," Harwant also joined in.

"She even found out who Sukhbir was and often visited him on her way to and from Chandigarh. She helped Sukhbir get married to Raj. We attended the wedding and she presented as the main wedding ceremonies organiser," Ninder suddenly became supportive.

"Sukhbir didn't even invite us to the wedding," Jessica said, surprisingly.

"Because Sukhbir thought that you, like your dad, would not allow you to marry a poor and low caste maid," said Ninder.

"Oh, my God! Do you think we are so backward?"

"Yes, Amrita thinks the villagers who went abroad did not change to a modern way of living. They still believe in old traditions and customs. She also thinks that it is absurd Jessica keeps on doubting her having an affair with Karan. Therefore, he does not pick up her phone," Harwant informed.

"I don't know why Amrita treats our family like hers. It's hard to understand her personality and her behaviour. I know some people are introverted like to be alone most of the time and prefer solitude. Some are extroverts and feel happy about going out and about and being around family and friends. Amrita does not fall into any category; she might have a borderline personality disorder or be a stalker. That is why her one-sided love for Karan is somewhat unexplainable," Jessica tried to make some sense out of it.

Sitting in the lounge, looking at each other silently to find the answer to a question, they became mentally tired of thinking about Amrita. Finally, Karan spoke about his usual dialogue.

"In this world and the universe, there are many things we don't know. We don't even know who we are and what this universe is all about, let alone God."

All laughed at this dialogue because they had heard this from him many times. Harwant laughed and said, "I know what this dialogue means—you need a shot of whiskey before bed."

They all came back into the lounge. Jessica sat quietly on the couch. Harwant updated them on their parent's condition, which was worsening.

They decided to visit their parents the next day and then Karan and Jessica would go for dinner at Jessica's Royal Castle.

Dinner at the Royal Palace

After seeing his parents, who were still fighting death, Karan and Jessica arrived at the Royal Castle in the evening. It was an old royal palace belonging to Amrita's great-grandfather, who inherited it from his king's ancestry.

Amrita's parents inherited it from their parents and they decorated it to a very high standard and made it a luxurious palace. It was a large property with vast gardens, meadows, lakes and acres of farming land. The king used to come here for hunting and celebrate festive seasons in the Royal Banquet Hall in this palace.

The castle had long green lawns surrounding it. Various green trees and shrubs grew on the sides of the long country drive to the castle. The drive led to an extensive round frontage with a fountain in the centre at the driveway's end. The small round water reservoir around contained red fish swimming. On the left was a car garage for three or four cars. An old Morgan sports car and a vintage Rolls Royce were parked in front of the garage.

The main entrance led to a wide hallway with large paintings on the walls in golden frames. On the side of the hallway were two large lounges on either side, which had huge paintings hanging on the wall. In both lounges, there were big fireplaces built on the front walls and above the mantel, surface hung large mirrors with golden frames and deer heads on either side of the mirrors.

In front of the fireplace was a lion's skin with a lion's head laid on a beautiful Arabian rug. The hallway opened into a large banquet hall fully decorated royal style with wide cobbing, large pillars and giant chandeliers. The walls of this hall were half covered with mahogany wood.

Again, there were large paintings on the walls and engraved pictures on the ceiling. Behind the right-sided lounge was a large dining hall with a double door opening into the hall. Behind the hall on the left was an old library with old volumes of books.

In the library's centre were a large writing mahogany desk and a red leather chair. On one side was a relaxing chair to sit comfortably to read. The banquet hall opened directly to the back lawn with a double door. On the side of the library was a small room called the Gunroom, which had rifles and a pistol for hunting. In front, there was a hallway leading to horse stables and horse riding pathways in the back gardens.

In the middle of the hallway was a wide wooden staircase leading to the upstairs landing and hallway. A large chandelier was hanging from the ceiling in the middle of the stairs. Around the upstairs hallway were at least ten large bedrooms, each with an en-suite.

Amrita's father, Kanwar Pratap Singh, was a retired Colonel from the British army. He had learnt to shoot 'Clay Pigeon' from his fellow British army officers. Horse riding and clay pigeon shooting had become his hobby; he often played this with Manav's dad, Amritpal Singh.

Manav had moved in with his in-laws after marriage because Amrita wanted to stay with her parents to live the royal life. Amrita, the only daughter, was going to inherit the entire estate; therefore, it was a wise decision on her part. Manav and Amrita lived there but were entirely independent to live their own life.

As a socialite, Manav was not happy living in the palace and he always expressed his dissatisfaction with Karan, "Palaces, big cars, not everything in life, friend, improving the lives of poor people is my mission!"

Manav's family got along well with Amrita's family. Their dads were good friends and they could discuss military battlefields and politics over whiskey drinking and chess sessions.

Karan was terrified to meet Amrita's parents because of what had happened in the past. He thought they might still talk about Amrita's wanting to marry him and insult him.

"Hello, Karan!" Amrita's dad extended his hand to shake hands, but Karan hesitated but joined hands together and said, "Hello, Colonel. We have to keep a social distance."

"Yes, boy. You are right."

"This is Jessica—my wife—" Karan introduces his wife.

"Jessica, you are beautiful—Amrita is always talking about you."

"Sir, we are very sorry about Manav. Please accept our condolence."

"It's a regrettable demise of an intelligent lad like Manav. It is regretful, but it was his fault for getting addicted to drugs and alcohol. He would have been a great leader if he didn't do that. Let's go inside." He also gestured to enter with his left hand.

Karan looked around and complimented the house, "Colonel Saheb, what a beautiful palace you have!"

"Thanks and thanks to my ancestors for this gift. I will take you to show this palace from the inside and outside. We will go on horseback to the lake and shoot clay pigeons. Can you fire a gun at all?" The Colonel was in his charming mood.

"Yes, a bit, as students in medical college. All students have training in NCC."

"The NCC?" Jessica asked.

"National Cadet Corps—this was army training to be a reservist cadet and it was mandatory to have this training in weaponry and army discipline. We had rifle training and weekly parades and must attend at least two army camps. The government could deploy reservists at times of war."

"I am sure you could not hit the target being a doctor—ha ha," Colonel laughed.

"It was always bulls-eye, Colonel, bulls-eye," Karan said confidently.

"We will see that soon. Let's have a drink first."

They had one whiskey each. Amrita brought her mother into a wheelchair.

"Mum, Karan and Jessica."

"Who are they?" Mum asked, rolling her eyes.

"Don't mind. Mum has dementia."

"Amrita! You never told me." Karan showed his concern.

Amrita decided not to answer this. Karan and Amrita remembered when her mother physically and mentally abused her when she wanted to marry Karan. Although it was known to the Colonel, he preferred not to open old wounds.

Before dinner, Colonel took Karan and Jessica around and Amrita went to the kitchen to instruct the chef on which food to prepare. Then she took Jessica to her bedroom. Colonel took Karan to the Gun Room. There were all kinds of guns and Karan felt uncomfortable because he had not used a gun after his NCC training.

The Colonel picked up two barrelled 12-bore shotguns, one for himself and the other he gave to Karan. Then they went to the stable and got two horses. Karan had learnt horse riding in the UK with his friends. They arrived at the lakeside. The Colonel had trained his horse keeper to fire clay pigeons via a trap machine. The Colonel had the first go and it was Karan's turn. The horse keeper flew a clay pigeon over the lake and Karen shot him with the first go. He then did the same for the second and third clay pigeons.

The Colonel was amazed and remarked, "Wonderful, well-done, Karan. I now know why Amrita always keeps praising you."

"As she must have told you, we were very close friends. We tried to excel at each other by praising each other's achievements." Karan avoided prolonging the discussion.

Colonel and Karan then had a horse ride around gardens and meadows and had a bit of a horse race. Amrita took Jessica to a different bedroom. Jessica saw a large picture of Karan and Manav on the dressing table in that bedroom. She had a garland of artificial flowers around Manav's photo, which signifies that the person had died.

In front of the pictures was a gold-plated tray on which there was an earthen pot filled with water, a lit candle and sweets. On the side table were two brides' Punjabi suits, one red and one pink. There were red bangles and other golden jewellery to wear. Jessica was shocked and asked, "What is this all about?"

"We are going to perform the ritual of Karvachauth."

"What is Karvachauth?"

"Karwa is a small earthen pot of water like the one in the tray and Chauth means 'Fourth' or the fourth day after the full moon, which falls in October. On this day, wives eat something before sunrise and fast all day till moonrise. The ladies perform the ritual to wish their husbands a long life. Karvachauth is mainly celebrated in North India. The wives of soldiers pray for their safe return from the warranty. Another reason is to welcome the newly married woman into the new family.

"During celebrations, women dressed like Indian brides and wore beautiful gold jewellery and red bangles on this day. The women who have been fasting all day sit together in a circle and worship, sing songs and dance. They do not eat during the day and are not allowed to do housework. The moon rises much later that night. When the moon rises, the fasting women eat food, rejoice and embrace each other as friends and sisters," Amrita gave information in half Punjabi and half English.

"It sounds like a lovely festival, but this is not the day to do Karvachauth," Jessica realised.

"It does not matter; I feel like celebrating this ritual with you and praying for Karan's long life."

Amrita dressed Jessica in a red suit like a new bride and herself in pink. They put on the jewellery and bangles and looked like brides. Amrita picked up the tray with the candle in front of Karan's photo and she started prayers for him with Jessica standing on her side. Then they came downstairs to the dining room, where Karen and Colonel were waiting for them.

They were taken aback and shouted jointly, "What is this nonsense act?" Colonel shouted.

"Karvachauth ritual." Amrita put sweets in Karan's mouth and wished him a long life. She asked Jessica to do the same.

"You know we don't believe in these old rituals." The Colonel was getting angry. He could not understand what Amrita had done when they were grieving Manav's death.

Sitting next to Karan, Amrita's mother started crying and remembering Manav and then she suddenly started laughing. Amrita started crying and then she laughed as well with her mother. Karan asked Jessica and Amrita to go upstairs and change their clothes. Jessica went to her bedroom. Amrita started making painful noises and slashing her wrists.

After changing her dress, Jessica went to Amrita's bedroom. She had broken all her wedding bangles on the dressing table, covered with blood. Amrita had Manav's old pistol in her hands and was still crying. Jessica thought she would commit suicide because of the shock from Manav's death. She immediately called the Colonel and Karen.

The Colonel came and hugged Amrita. Amrita was silent, then clung to Karan. Jessica again slowly pulled them apart and laid her on the bed. Karan looked at the slashed wrists and the wounds were not very deep. Karan asked for a first aid box and tightly cleaned and dressed the wounds. Colonel grabbed the pistol from her hand. Amrita quickly came back to her senses and seemed fine. They all went downstairs and had dinner in silence. No one dared to speak.

After dinner, Karen and Jessica said, "Goodbye. We better be going. Amrita, don't do this frightening act again." Karan said, passing by.

Amrita crookedly looked at Karan and then Jessica and pronounced, "Karan, don't worry. I'm not going to die alone."

Fear

On their way home, Karan and Jessica were frightened by what Amrita had done. Her words, 'Karan, don't worry, I'm not going to die alone' were making a loud noise in their ears. Both were silent and fearful and kept thinking about what she meant by her last sentence.

Jessica took the courage to ask Karan, "What did she mean, to kill someone like you before she gets killed?" Jessica asked.

"I don't know what she meant; it is all nonsense. I think she has gone crazy after Manav's death; she is insane," Karan tried to share the fear with Jessica.

"No, Manav's death does not seem to bother her. She is just crazy about you. She is free to come after you or me now that Manav has gone. I fear her now. I think she was threatening to kill you or me. Amrita's Karvachauth ceremony was pre-planned and she could have killed me with the pistol. Karan, I am sure that was her intention, but she could not because you and her parents were in that house. I'm so scared, let's go to the UK tomorrow. Please let's go," Jessica pleaded.

"Jessica, I'm scared too, after what we have seen today. You're right; she is a crazy stalker and harmful to us. Soon, we will know what will happen to my parents. Until that, we will stay. We should be beware of Amrita's moves and will not meet her from today onwards."

At last, Karan had come to his senses.

They came home exhausted and frightened and went straight to the bedroom. Karan instructed the driver to close the gate and return the car to Amrita. Harwant and Ninder had already gone to their bedrooms. Jessica clung to Karan in bed in fear. They tried to sleep, but Amrita's words came into their mind. They were already very fearful of Coronavirus and now frightened of the 'Amrita Virus' being more dangerous. Their parents' imminent death further compounded their fear.

To make matters worse, governments could declare lockdown again because of the second wave of the Corona pandemic. They feared they would be stranded in Amritsar. Due to this, they may lose their jobs.

Their fear turned to sorrow when Karan expressed his feelings about his parents, "Look, my father and mother are in critical condition and there is little hope of rescuing them. They made us doctors with their hard work and sacrifices. If we are not with them even at the end of life, then I will not be able to forgive myself for the rest of my life. My mother has always been my strength and my father my wisdom. My strong-minded Jessica, be brave and support me a little longer."

"I'm always with you, my darling. We will fight Corona as well as 'Amrita variants' together." Jessica gathered her strength.

"That's my girl that I know!" Karan kissed Jessica on the forehead and hugged her.

Early in the morning, Karan had a call from Amrita from the hospital that his mother had a stroke and was unconscious. Father was having difficulty in breathing. Karan, Jessica and Harwant were rushed to the hospital. Amrita had already put his father and mother on a ventilator in the ICU. Karan assured Jessica that Amrita would treat his parents according to the current guidelines.

They arrived at the ICU wearing protective gowns and masks. They were not allowed to go into the ICU under restrictions. They saw their father and mother through a large mirror on the room's wall. Harwant and Karan had a heartfelt desire to be on the side of their parents' beds. The helplessness was unbearable. Amrita then brought their parents' records to show and discuss with Karan and Jessica. They looked at the ongoing treatment and Amrita explained everything like a senior professional doctor.

She informed, "As you know, COVID or the vaccine causes blood clots in the brain and lungs, which have happened to the father and mother. Both are receiving standard treatment, such as an oxygen ventilator, Ramdazvir, steroids and chest physio."

"You're providing the right treatment and care, thanks," said Jessica.

"Can we go in for two minutes, Amrita? You know we both work in similar circumstances in the UK?" Karan pleaded.

"Look, it's not safe."

"We are in full PPE."

Amrita let them go inside because they were senior doctors and worked in the ICU in the UK. Jessica made sure they were in full gear PPE before going inside. Father opened his eyes. He was given assisted oxygen with the ventilator and could not speak, but Karan could read his lips and body language.

"Save us, Karan. We made you all doctors with such hard work. Please do something, save us, please," the father was pleading to his children.

"Don't worry, dad—Amrita is taking good care of you and also seeks advice from us—you will be fine," Karan tried to console his father but knew they were on the death door.

They all agreed there was no point in resuscitating their parents when the end came. They should be kept on a ventilator in case they pull through. They knew mother would not survive. All she needed was tender, loving care. As they couldn't stay in the hospital long, they returned home.

Amrita was looking after them day and night. Despite good care, they died and Corona also took their life. Amrita broke the bad news on the phone to Karan, "Karan—I'm sorry—I couldn't save your mum and dad. You know, Mum was in a coma but became restless as if she was struggling to stay alive right at the end. Dad had difficulty breathing, which was not improving. Finally, father just gave up and stopped breathing. I am sorry I couldn't save them. I am so sad and can't express my sorrow in words. You know, I also considered them as my mum and dad."

After hearing the news, Karan, Harwant and Ninder got together. They all cried for some time. Jessica then started consoling everyone. They were very sad and grief-stricken. They realised that they must organise cremation and religious funeral services as soon as possible. There were long queues for a place in the crematorium.

Harwant being well-known in the community and having some connections, managed to get early cremation. Only ten people were allowed to attend the funeral. They cremated their parents according to the Sikh religious customs. The next day, five priests brought the holy book of Guru Granth Saheb into their house to perform a service called 'Akhund Path' and recited the whole of the sacred text to the family.

Jessica asked, "What is Akhund Path?"

"This Sikh religious service Akhund Path is a nonstop recitation of all verses in holy books in three days. It is supposed to destroy evil by worshipping God. It also brings peace and tranquillity to the bereaved family. The final prayer is undertaken on the third day, wishing their parents to rest in peace. The final prayer concludes the funeral ceremony," Ninder explained to Jessica.

After the Akhund Path was over, they garlanded big pictures of the father and mother and hung them together in the lounge.

Visit Holy Golden Temple

The Gurdwara administrative committee eased restrictions for the devotees to visit the Golden Temple. But devotees had to have face covers and keep a social distance. There were long queues in the temple. The committee had made special arrangements for queues.

In mourning and grief-stricken family decided to pay a visit to the Golden Temple. Everyone agreed to pray for their elders to rest in peace and to bring back happiness. Although Jessica wanted to return to the UK immediately, she always wanted to see the Golden Temple. It would not be customary if a person belonging to the Sikh religion did not pay such a visit. Karan had already given Jessica a lot of information about this holy place and she seemed eager to pay her respect.

The next thing was to choose appropriate timings because about a hundred thousand people visit this place daily. According to the United Nations data Golden Temple is the most visited place in the world.

Therefore, they chose four o'clock the following morning when there would be a small number of devotees. At that time, a religious procession called 'Prakash' meant "light," bringing the holy book, Guru Granth, from its resting place to the sanctum. Guru Granth Saheb is taken out of its bedroom, carried on the head and placed in a flower-decorated chariot called palki with chanting and bugle sounding across the causeway.

They went to the Golden Temple early, so they had enough time to go around the Parkarma, a marble path surrounding the Sarovar. They parked their car in a car park away from the temple. They walked through a long drive with many shops selling religious and sick traditional gifts and books. The 'famous Jalliaan Waal Bag' was in one corner of the drive.

At this place, many innocent people celebrating the Baisakhi festival were shot down by Colonel Reginald Edward Harry Dyer in 1919. The British thought it was a protest against Rowlatt Act and the Indians demanding freedom. Ninety soldiers, under his command, surrounded the Jallianwala Bagh and opened fire into the crowd.

They arrived at the big marble square in front of the front gate. On the left was a place to deposit shoes and socks before entering. Everyone was surprised to see Amrita and her dad waiting for them. Amrita again took charge and ordered, "Everyone remove your shoes and socks and I will deposit this myself."

They all did that. Amrita took all shoes and socks and gave these to people working there, free to deposit in the shoe cupboards. She collected a token with a cupboard number on it. She then asked, "Have you all got your headcovers?"

She took one from her bag and gave it to Karan and pointed, "I knew you wouldn't bring one."

Harwant and Ninder looked at each other and grinned. All men covered their heads with handkerchiefs and women with their scarves. Jessica half covered her head, but Amrita pulled it forward to cover the whole of her head. She then led them to the front gate. Colonel prompted, "You must wash your hands and feet before you go in."

They entered the gateway and at the end, there were steps to the Parkarma. The Golden Temple was built below the ground level to show that this religion preaches modesty. Before they took steps to Parkarma, Jessica was overwhelmed by the sheer religious feeling of looking at the Golden Temple.

It was glittering in gold, with its shadow in the holy water was breathtaking. The atmosphere was holy, peaceful, clean and serene. She kept standing there and folded her hands and chanted, Satnam, Waheguru. Karan looked at her beautiful wife, who looked like a pure religious devotee. He got his camera out and wanted to take her picture and she declined by saying, "Let me enjoy this holly feeling in my mind and soul first."

"Let us go. We will be late for the procession; have you got special permission to attend?" Colonel asked.

"No, we didn't know that." Everyone was surprised.

"Don't worry. My dad had got permission for everyone," informed Amrita.

They went down the steps and knelt with their forehead, touching Parkarma to pay respect to the Golden Temple. This act 'Matha Takana', meaning touching the ground with the forehead in front of any religious place or holy book.

They started the circumambulation of Parkarma. The religious singers Hazoori Ragis in the sanctum sang hymns broadcasted around the Golden Temple and worldwide. One could hear them all around the temple. Giant television screens showed translated hymns in English on each corner of the Parkarma. The hymn being sung meant, "Why downgrade a woman when she gives birth even to kings? Women are equal to men. They are our friends and love."

"What are those two tall towers?" Jessica asked.

"These are called Ramgarhia Bungas. These towers were built in the 18th century during Afghan attacks to demolish the temple. These are named after the Ramgarhia Sikh warriors. From the top of the towers, the security guards watch for any military raid approaching the temple," Colonel explained.

They passed the towers and saw a tree on the bank of the Sarovar where devotees were having a dip in the holy water. Amrita told Jessica, "This tree is called Dukh Bhanjani Ber. In this place, a Sikh was cured of his leprosy after taking a dip in the pool. After this, the tree became the epithet of "suffering and sins remover"."

"Amrita, you should dip in this holy water," Jessica said sarcastically.

Amrita never expected that nasty sarcasm but went quiet. They carried on walking and passed the second and the third entrance. They reached Darshani Deori, the main entrance to the sanctum. The Prakash ceremony was going on. They were allowed just inside the entrance and when the procession passed, they followed it to the sanctum.

They bowed at the entrance of the Sanctum and went in. The holy book was rested in its place. The head priest opened the holy book and recited a hymn which became the thought for that day. They stayed in the sanctum and walked around and went upstairs. They all felt spiritual awareness.

All of them completed the rest of the Parkarma and came out. This time Amrita collected the shoes. They then briefly saw the Sikh museum. The display shows various paintings of gurus and martyrs and historical items. The new underground museum outside the temple courtyard also shows Sikh history. They paid a brief visit to Jillian Wala Bag, which was upsetting. They came out of the Bag and said goodbye to Amrita and her father.

Amria could not handle this departure. She hugged Jessica and Karan and said, "Goodbye. Have a safe journey to the UK. God willing, we shall be meeting again."

Back in the UK

Karan and Jessica wanted to return to work quickly, so they booked the first flight to London. They boarded the plane a few days after Karan's parents' funeral.

When they arrived at Heathrow airport, they had to stay in a government-sanctioned hotel for a fortnight quarantine at his own expense. Their son Theo had come to pick them up, but he had to return to Leicester. They informed their hospital about it. After the quarantine was complete, Theo returned to pick them up. They met at the arrival and looked very sad, even with masks on their faces and started shedding tears.

"Dad, I am sorry we lost my grandma and grandpas," he cried over her mother's shoulder and his father hugged him. They were silent throughout the whole journey home. They arrived home and Karen hung the picture of his parents and his father-in-law and put artificial flowers around each photo.

In the UK, thousands of people are dying every day from COVID-19. Many blamed the government's decision to relax lockdowns. UK government had to impose a complete lockdown test and tracing program was expanded and the government created a new minister for vaccination. This program was successful and millions of vaccines were given every day.

In their daily bulletin, the chief medical officer recommended two doses of vaccines, the first one straight, the other three months later and a booster three to six months. The pandemic was slowly coming under control.

Jessica reported to work and immediately started working in their department. Jessica took charge of the ICU, full of patients needing ventilators. Karan began working as posted in the acute COVID ward, where the patients needed initial admission. Theo had been working in another hospital as a junior doctor. He was so busy that sometimes he had to do overtime. Even though they had two vaccination doses, they were still at risk of catching COVID.

One day while working, Jessica began to feel weak. The next day, she had a fever and cough. The taste in the mouth and the sense of smell had disappeared. Karan did the test for Corona and it was positive. Her condition deteriorated in a few days and he admitted her to her hospital. X-rays of the lungs showed COVID-related pneumonia. Her breathing was difficult and there was a decline in oxygen saturation, so she was moved to ICU and put on a ventilator.

Karan could not believe this was happening to his family. Jessica had standard treatment for COVID. Karan stayed around the ICU until the evening but hanging around was no point. He decided to come home. He was very anxious and frightened. There was no one at home. Theo was working all day in London. He could hardly talk to him on the phone, as he was constantly busy with patients.

Karan being a contact, had to isolate himself at home for two weeks. First, he informed Harwant, his brother in India, about Jessica, who could not say anything apart from consoling him. He was desperate to talk to someone. In this panic situation, he called Amrita, "Amrita—I can't believe Jessica has got Corona. She is on the ventilator but stable, but I am frightened."

"Don't worry—I am sure she being young, will pull through. She must be having the best treatment in England. Just be brave like you used to be. Remember, I am always there to help."

"After all the deaths in our family and Jessica in the ICU with COVID, I'm shattered and feeling down. I don't know how I am going to cope."

"Look—you know how much I love you; my soul dwells in yours. Use it to find strength. You are strong. Don't worry; whatever happens, I will look after you all your life."

"Stop talking nonsense—you have already started thinking the unthinkable. I firmly believe my Jessica will get better and never leave me," he said as he hung up.

One morning, Karan was having breakfast and calling the hospital to check Jessica's condition when the doorbell rang. He opened the door and could not believe it was Amrita on his doorstep.

"Oh, my God—Amrita, I can't believe you have come here as well?"

"Karan, I have told you many times I will be with you through thick and thin. I have come to help you with this situation. We'll get Jessica better together. Let me in and which way is your guest room?" She went upstairs to the guest room straightway. She unpacked her luggage, put her clothes in the wardrobe and made herself comfortable.

Karan was stunned and wanted to kick her out of the house immediately, but for old friendship's sake, he showed a curtsy. He decided to keep his distance from her and call her daughter, Anamika, to come and be with her mother. He knew Amrita had come to do some harm and was very cautious about his safety. Anamika had to apply for annual leave, but she could not come straightway. There were a few days left in Karan's isolation.

He felt like he was on lockdown in his own house and haunted by the Amrita Virus, which might cause death. He took all the precautions and hoped she would not do anything terrible. Amrita came down with presents and pulses she had brought from India. She wanted to cook Karan's favourite Indian Curry and Dal. She came to the kitchen and started cooking.

She shouted from the kitchen so that Karan could hear, "I am cooking your favourite Dal and curry, which you like."

Karan, sitting in the study, was planning how to get rid of Amrita. He decided to send her with her daughter to London. He decided to discuss it with Amrita over dinner.

"Amrita, you shouldn't have come here."

"Why are you still scared of Jessica? Don't worry. I am not going to kill anyone. I am already dead because I can't have your love."

"Amrita, you are a prestigious doctor and princess, don't be silly saying such immoral things. I don't like you coming to my home when Jessica is so ill. You go with your daughter to spend your break with her."

"Is this how you treat your dear friends? You should at least appreciate my love for you. Keep me with you for a few days and then I will go to London with my daughter, Anamika. When Jessica gets well and comes home, I want to meet her before I go to London and then to India."

"All right, but you have to leave."

"OK—come on, don't look so scared. Let us remember good times. I want to have a drink with you as you used to do with my husband," Amrita insisted, grabbed his hand and led him upstairs to the bar. She stood behind the bar and poured whiskey into a crystal glass for Karan and Gin with Tonic water. She asked Karan to bring ice from the fridge downstairs in the kitchen.

When he went downstairs, she spiked his whiskey with the drug ketamine. She had pinched it from her anaesthesia department in India. Karan brought ice cubes and lemons for a gin and tonic drink. Amrita gave Karan his glass to him. She picked up her drink and spoke, "Cheers, toast to Manav and our friendship."

They downed the first drink in one gulp. Jessica then made another drink for both. Karan was already drunk and started staggering. Soon, he was in a semi-comatose state. Amrita grabbed him and took him to his bedroom.

Ketamine is used as an anaesthetic before an operation and makes a person unconscious. But Amrita had given the dose which would keep him in a semi-coma for a few hours. Amrita stole Jessica's sexy nightie, groomed herself to look beautiful and then put bangles used for the wedding in her arms. She had a massive amount of red lipstick. She grabbed Manav's revolver she had brought from India in one hand and the Kamasutra book in the other.

She laid over Karan's half-unconscious body and took all his clothes off. Karan opened his eyes and thought the woman over him was Jessica; he kissed her and asked, "Jessica, are you OK—why are you bearing these wedding bangles? I wouldn't say I like these bangles around your arms. These remind me you are locked elsewhere in the ICU. Is lockdown alpha still on? When did you come back from heaven? He kept muttering nonsensically."

Amrita took her nightie off and laid on his naked body, kissing him on the lips and the body to arouse him sexually and reassure him.

"Yeah—I'm your Jessica—I'm fine—Let's make love."

"Take your bangles off. I don't like them on your wrists," he murmured again.

Amrita banged her bangles against the side of the bed and broke them. She started rolling the revolver on his head and demanded Karan to make love; otherwise, she would kill him. With extended foreplay, she aroused Karan and opened the pages of Kamasutra Asanas, called sexual positions and made love in each position.

She carried on until they reached climax. Karan went to sleep, completely paralysed because of the ketamine spiking of his drink. There was a deep satisfaction on Amrita's face as if she had fulfilled her lifelong desire to have sex with Karan. He looked at Karan, who was in a deep sleep and smiled at him.

Putting her revolver in her handbag, she remembered how she had cleverly got it through security in India. She started flirting with the security officer and distracted him when her handbag containing Manav's revolver went through the scan.

The doorbell rang loudly and Amrita went downstairs and opened the door. There stood four gipsies, one of whom was a gipsy girl.

"Madam, we are travellers and we have set up our camp with our caravans in your fields with the permission of doctor Karanveer Singh. We have a wedding coming and intend to use your abandoned church for this and then we agreed to move on."

"Travellers, what do you mean?"

"Madam, we used to be called 'Gypsies', but now we are called 'Travellers' in a civilised way."

"Yes, what do you want?"

"We need the keys to the catholic church across the river. It is in a derelict state and we will make it good and decorate it for Joseph and Marion's wedding. The doctor has already agreed to it."

"That's good! Let me find the keys."

The church keys were hanging on the key hanger in the hallways with a church tag. She took the keys and said, "I have never seen what the church looks like from the inside. I want to come with you."

The church had not been used for a long time. Previously, people who lived in the house had built a small private church for them. The church had two rows of wooden benches for seating about fifteen people. There was a stage with steps to go up the stage. At the back of the stage, there was an altar for prayer. On the wall behind the altar was a picture of Jesus and Mary.

On one side of the stage, steps went down to a wooden called a confession chamber.

"What is this confession chambers?" Amrita asked Joseph.

"The confession chamber is for the priest to sit inside with the door closed. He then hears the confessions of sins by penitents. This chamber has holes on the side through which the pertinent confess sins to the priest, giving his blessing in return."

Amrita seemed very interested in the confession chamber, which has a door and lock. Amrita found a key to the chamber, opened the door and examined it and its surroundings thoroughly. Then she locked it again. She handed the keys to Joseph and said, "All the best for your wedding. Bring the keys over when you finish."

She returned home and found Karan was still fast asleep and unconscious. He got up a few hours later. Karan saw his dirty linen and broken bangles all around. He looked at his naked body, which was full of red lipstick marks and realised that Amrita had made love to him after getting him drunk. He got up and went to Amrita's room. She, too, was fast asleep. He returned to his room and looked at his bed and broken bangles again.

"Oh, my God! Amrita made me drink and—"

He was very angry with himself for letting it happen. He immediately cleared the room and changed the linen on the bed. He felt like he was raped and had a long shower. He washed his body again and again.; but could not wash away the immorality with soap.. He still had a hangover, so he went to bed and slept deeply. Amrita woke up and saw that Karan was asleep. She called a taxi according to her plan.

"Let's visit Jessica in the hospital," she planned something very nasty.

On arriving ICU, Amrita put on full PPE. She took Jessica's name badge and wrote her name on it. She was familiar with the functioning of the ICU and acted as a locum consultant for Jessica. The ICU charge nurse looked at his badge and asked, "Doctor, are you covering for Jessica?"

"Yes, nurse, take me to Jessica."

The nurse took her to Jessica's room. A junior doctor and the other nurses were caring for her. Amrita introduced herself in such a way that everyone believed her. She examined Jessica and then looked at her observations and treatment chart. She asked the doctor how she had been and discussed further treatment professionally. Jessica was also trying to cough out the secretions in her pipe but could not.

Amrita asked the nurses for a suction machine and she sucked jelly-like saliva from the tracheal tube and beyond. She cleared the lungs and the tracheal tube, which improved Jessica's breathing. This improved oxygen saturation and Jessica stopped coughing. A patient in the adjoining room deteriorated and she sent a doctor and nurses to attend to that patient.

It was the perfect time to kill Jessica from a natural cause. She disconnected the tracheal tube from the ventilator, introducing oxygen to the lungs. Within a minute, Jessica was breathing heavily and her heart started fibrillating. She became unconscious. The nurses at the monitor station noticed Jessica's trace, which showed heart fibrillation and put an emergency call to the resuscitation team.

Before the team arrived, Amrita connected the breathing tube to the ventilator and started compressions of the chest. The resuscitation team leader took over and Amrita sneaked out, announcing she would attend to the other patients. The team leader provided electric shock a couple of times while others continued with chest compressions.

Jessica's heart started beating normally. Her breathing improved and Jessica regained consciousness. She woke up and became agitated. Jessica pulled out the tracheal tube and started breathing normally but had a croaky voice. The anaesthetist in the team wanted to put back the tracheal tube and connect to the ventilator, but Jessica stopped him as she could breathe normally. She asked for a steroid injection to reduce the swelling of inside lining of the trachea and voice box.

Amrita knew that sometimes there was swelling inside the windpipe being on the ventilator. She already had her lung secretions sucked by Amrita. Her breathing without the ventilator improved remarkably and her blood oxygen saturation was normal. Her heart remained in normal rhythm.

After knowing Jessica's resuscitation was successful, Amrita slipped out of the ICU and arrived home as if nothing had happened. Amrita did not manage to kill Jessica. The doctor called Karan to inform him that his wife had a successful resuscitation. She had survived COVID and was fully conscious and off the ventilator.

When Amrita arrived home, she saw Karan was doped but very happy. He wanted to share the good news about Jessica. He informed her.

"Amrita, Jessica is off the ventilator and breathing fine without the ventilator."

"I know—I already know."

"How do you know?"

"While you were asleep, I visited her in the ICU. I noticed her tracheal tube was disconnected. Jessica stopped breathing. Immediately, she went into cardiac arrest. I was able to cardiovert her heart to a normal rhythm. She was uncomfortable with the tracheal tube she pulled out. Because of my help, she is breathing perfectly normally."

"You put on Jessica's green scrub suit and used her badge to get into the ICU," Karan asked in surprise.

"That's why they let me in. When I told them that I was locum to cover Jessica, they let me see Jessica."

"You are a cunning devil, Amrita."

"I promised to always be there for you when you need me. Look, l have proved to you that I care about you. Have you seen dirty bed linen and broken bangles in your bedroom? After getting drunk, you had forced sex with me. I had to fight with you and you broke my bangles."

Karan was ashamed of himself because Amrita convinced him she was not as bad. He felt sorry and he requested her, "Well, Amrita, I am very sorry, the drink just had gone to my head. Could you please keep my misbehaviour to yourself?"

"Of course, I can do anything for you, my darling," Amrita said with sarcasm.

A few days later, Jessica came home after discharge from the hospital. She was surprised to see Amrita at her home. Karan told Jessica that she was there to help us. He also told her how Amrita enabled her to revive in ICU.

After knowing this, Jessica was thankful to her and accepted her stay. Happiness has returned home after a long time. Theo also came home because there was no need for a doctor at the temporary COVID ward. Amrita's daughter Anamika had also arrived there. Even though Karan felt guilty inside, he was putting everything behind him and showing his unconditional love to Jessica. Jessica could now tolerate Amrita. They were now spending quite a bit of time together.

One day Jessica asked, "What did you tell me about Karvachauth?"

"On Karvachauth day, women fast on the fourth day of the full moon and pray to God for their husbands' longevity. They take sweets and food, go to temples or gurdwaras and pray. When the moon rises at night, they break their fast by eating sweets and food," explained Amrita.

"I also want to do Karvachauth fast for Karan," said Jessica in excitement.

"Jessica, this is neither the day of Karvachauth nor is there any Gurdwara or temple here."

"It does not matter. We will fast and go to our private church. I hope it has been cleaned and decorated by travellers. I don't care if it is not on the day of Karvachauth."

"OK, we'll both fast for Karan," she said, laughing, but Jessica was not amused.

Karan and Theo had returned to work at the hospital to carry on their war against COVID. Jessica took Amrita and Anamika shopping in Leicester. They bought Indian suits, one pink and the other red. They also bought jewellery, bangles, Indian sweets and other things for Karvachauth.

The following day, Jessica wore a red suit. Amrita wore a pink suit with jewellery and bangles. They looked like brides. They enjoyed listening to Bollywood and Karvachauth songs all day long. The daughter also started singing with them. The days are longer in summer in England. Anamika decided to meet her friend in Nottingham and stay there overnight.

Jessica and Amrita both went to church. They put all ingredients on two plates. Amrita brought with her a picture of Guru Nanak. Jessica was born and raised in England.

She had her early education in Catholic Schools; therefore, she knew all the hymns and prayers from the Bible. They laid the trays containing candles and sweets on the altar. Amrita also put the photo of Guru Nanak. Amrita recited five verses of Japji Saheb, which she knew by heart. They both prayed for Karan's long life. Finally, they put the sweets in each other's mouths. Amrita then took Jessica to the confession chamber.

She asked Amrita, "Come here. I wonder what this little chamber is for?"

"Catholics tell the priest about their sins and pray to God for forgiveness," said Jessica.

"Well, I need to confess my sins, as there is no priest. Will you go in the chamber and pretend to be my pastor?"

But the purpose of Amrita was different. As soon as Jessica went in, she locked the door. She shouted, "Now you are in proper lockdown until you die of Amrita Virus."

"Amrita, please don't do that. I am your friend; for God's sake, don't do this horrible thing. Please unlock me," Jessica begged.

Jessica started shouting and banging the confession chamber, "Help, help—help someone. Jessica has locked me in this chamber and wants to kill me."

Jessica ignored her and walked out of the church and locked it and murmured, "That will teach you, stupid woman, snatching my lifelong love Karan from me. You shouldn't have brought Karan to the UK and locked him in your jail forever. Now you will die in this chamber. No one will find out and I will take Karan to India and release him from your lockdown."

Amrita then started screaming like a crazy woman and felt victorious in taking her revenge. She threw all the keys to the church into the river. When Karan and Theo came home, they found Jessica was not home. Amrita came down after changing clothes. Karan and Theo asked her.

"Where's Jessica?" Karan asked.

"Jessica told me she is going to meet a friend and took Anamika to Nottingham with her. Anamika was going to stay with her friend overnight, but Jessica was coming back, but she had not returned. I'm worried about her. I hope she is not involved in an accident. I have already rung my daughter, but she is not picking up her phone." Amrita played her false innocence.

Jessica, as usual, had left her cell phone at home.

"You don't know the address of your daughter's friend?"

"I'm so stupid—I should have asked."

"Dad, what should we do?" Theo expressed concern.

"Look at the computer to see if she has been to any accident and emergency departments."

"I have already done so; she is not admitted to hospitals."

"Dad! Mum is missing. Shall I call the police?" Theo was anxious.

Karan picked up the phone and spoke to the police. Karan told them about missing Jessica, but their answer was, "We call someone a 'missing person' if they are missing for twenty-four hours—you call in the morning if your wife does not return home. Then we will start the search. She is an adult person; she will return."

They stayed up all night, but Amrita fell asleep in her room. Jessica did not return by the morning.

"Dad! How much do you know about Amrita?" Theo was suspicious of Amrita.

"She has been our friend for a long time. She loved me and it was one-sided love. I never loved her and according to your mum, she is a stalker and after us to do some harm. She might be here to harm your mum," Karan told Theo everything about his past life.

"Dad, I fear Amrita has something to do with mums missing. I hope she has not thrown Mum in the river."

"Maybe—but what if this suspicion turned out wrong?"

They kept calling their friends, relatives and hospitals all night, but no one could find Jessica. Karan called the police again, but they repeated what they had already told him. It was morning. The doorbell rang and they ran to open the door. The gipsies were standing outside and told them, "Sir! We have come to collect the keys for the final decorations of the church. We think somebody in here in the church and we could hear some knocking inside the church and someone shouting for help."

They immediately guessed it was Jessica locked inside. There were no keys on the key hanger. Karan shouted, "Amrita, did you lock Jessica in the church?"

"Yes, that's what I did and I have come here to kill her." Amrita had old Manav's pistol aiming at them.

"Give me the keys to the church—please, for the sake of your love." Karan pretended to show his love.

"OK, but tell me the truth about whether you love me. If you love me, tell me again. I will go to church with you and release Jessica." Amrita had the same gun aiming at Karan.

"Yes, my darling—I love you," Karan pretended.

"But I have thrown the church keys into the river." She asked them to follow to the church with a revolver butting into Karen's back.

Theo was observing as they arrived at the church door. He then ran to the side of the church. While playing in childhood, Theo discovered a small stair down to a narrow back door. There he called the police and explained the emergency. Police arrived in with full armour gear immediately.

Amrita asked the gipsies to break the lock, but they hesitated. A policeman brought a crowbar from the car and split the safety. With a revolver pushed against Karen's chest wall, Jessica shouted for him to enter the church. The police also targeted their guns on Jessica and asked her to let Karan go. She ignored the warnings and instructed Karan to the confession chamber, where Jessica shouted for help. Some policemen had entered the back door and had their guns ready to fire.

The travellers were frightened and were using a sign of the cross in front of their chest and said, "Jesus! save the lady and everyone."

"Break the door of the chamber," Amrita ordered Karan.

He broke the door by banging his foot. Jessica called Karan to enter the confession chamber to sit with Jessica. She ordered loudly, "Now confess that you love me in front of your wife. Then apologise for your infidelity."

Jessica was weak and carried on saying to the police, "Please help us and please save us."

Amrita, aiming her gun at both, ordered Karen again.

"Confess that you only love me. You betrayed me by loving Jessica; you must apologise in front of everyone; otherwise, I will kill Jessica. I went to the hospital to cut her oxygen supply through the ventilator, but I couldn't kill her, but she will die today with my bullet."

Amrita fired her pistol on the side wall of the chamber and screamed, "Confess that you love me."

Karan looked at Jessica affectionately and remembered when he saw her for the first time and fell in love with her. Looking at her, he was ready to die. He had the feeling Amrita would shoot them both.

"Amrita, I am ready to confess and apologise. I want to do this in front of everyone outside the chamber."

Amrita agreed and as soon as they came out, she started hitting both with her revolver head. A policeman had been posted behind the chamber. Amrita's daughter Anamika had also returned. Theo told her everything. She was crying and shouting at her mum, "Mum, don't do it. Let uncle and Auntie go, please."

"Oh no, I am going to kill them," Amrita flatly refused.

Karan took courage and looked at Amrita's face and he spoke truthfully, loud and clear to Amrita, "Amrita! I had never loved you, nor do I now and will never love you. I only love Jessica. If you want to kill us, do it." Karan hid Jessica behind him.

Amrita turned her revolver on Jessica and started crying.

"I have been cheated all my life—you have been lying all your life." Saying this, she put a revolver above her right ear and shot herself.

Falling on the floor, Amrita said, "No matter what, Karan, I will keep on loving you. Now I have unlocked you and Jessica. Goodbye, now, but trust me, I will be back; my desires compel me."

The ambulance has arrived. The paramedics tried to resuscitate Amrita, but it was unsuccessful. Amrita was declared dead. The ambulance crew then took her to a nearby hospital for confirming death by doctors. Jessica, Karan and Theo embraced and kissed each other. They came back to the lounge in their home. The prime minister was happily reporting on television the daily bulletin, "I am happy to share that we have succeeded in containing the COVID pandemic. We have lifted Lockdown Alpha."

Amrita's daughter Anamika was crying and looking at Theo, hoping for a big, lovely hug.